Bread Loaf

Writers' Conference

August 9-20, 1995

Michael Collier, Director
Devon Jersild, Administrative Director

Fiction: Charles Baxter, Cynthia Kadohata, Pablo Medina, Kevin McIlvoy, Reginald McKnight, Valerie Miner, C.E. Poverman, Francine Prose, Helen Schulman, Joanna Scott

Poetry: Michael Collier, Cornelius Eady, Jorie Graham, Edward Hirsch, Heather McHugh, Alberto Rios, Ellen Bryant Voigt

Nonfiction: Patricia Hampl, Alec Wilkinson, Terry Tempest Williams

Special Guest Reader: William Maxwell

For information and application materials, please write to: Mrs. Carol Knauss, The Bread Loaf Writers' Conference, Middlebury College – GS, Middlebury VT 05753-6111, or telephone (802) 388-3711, extension 5286.

THE 1994 1995 PUSHCART PRIZE XIX

BEST OF THE SMALL PRESSES

EDITED BY
BILL HENDERSON
WITH THE
PUSHCART PRIZE
EDITORS

630 PAGES
$29.50
HARDBOUND
JUST PUBLISHED

PUSHCART PRESS
P.O. BOX 380
WAINSCOTT, N.Y. 11975

"It's hard not to get too excited about the latest enormous volume of the best of the noncommercial world of short stories, poetry and essays...a surprising, vital collection that should hearten all serious readers."

Kirkus Reviews

"It just keeps getting bigger (630 pages) and better...this collection is more than just a recommended purchase. It's mandatory."

Library Journal

"A truly remarkable collection...small presses continue to be a bastion of excellence in the increasingly sloppy world of commercial publishing."

Booklist

"Pushcart's nineteenth anthology from a year's worth of American small press publishing is striking in its literary breadth and accomplishment...There is so much to choose from here that readers may not want to choose at all—they can just read on and on."

Publishers Weekly (starred review)

Turns you on to Art

Subscribe now! 636 Broadway 12th floor
New York, NY 10012 Tel: (212) 673 2660 Fax (212) 673 2887

GRAND STREET

Games

52

Front cover: Robert Williams, *Lord High Solver Of Puzzledom*, 1990
Back cover: Jay DeFeo, *Untitled (Egyptian Collage)*, no date (c.1956)

"A Deep-Sea Explorer of the Mind" is excerpted from *I Don't Want To Be Inside Me Anymore* by Birger Sellin. Copyright © 1995 by BasicBooks. Reprinted with permission of BasicBooks, a division of HarperCollins Publishers, Inc.

Grand Street (ISBN 1-885490-03-8) is published quarterly by Grand Street Press (a project of the New York Foundation for the Arts, Inc., a not-for-profit corporation), 131 Varick Street, Room 906, New York, N.Y. 10013. Contributions and gifts to Grand Street Press are tax-deductible to the extent allowed by law. This publication is made possible, in part, by a grant from the National Endowment for the Arts.

Second-class postage paid at New York, N.Y. and additional mailing offices. Postmaster: Please send address changes to Grand Street Subscription Service, Dept. GRS, P.O. Box 3000, Denville, N.J. 07834. Subscriptions are $40 a year (four issues). Foreign subscriptions (including Canada) are $55 a year, payable in U.S. funds. Single-copy price is $12.95 ($15 in Canada). For subscription inquiries, please call (800) 807-6548.

Grand Street is printed by the Studley Press in Dalton, MA. It is distributed to the trade by D.A.P./Distributed Art Publishers, 636 Broadway, 12th floor, New York, N.Y. 10012, Tel: (212) 473-5119, Fax: (212) 673-2887, and to newsstands only by B. DeBoer, Inc., 113 E. Centre Street, Nutley, N.J. 07110 and Fine Print Distributors, 6448 Highway 290 E., Austin, TX 78723. *Grand Street* is distributed in Australia and New Zealand by Peribo Pty, Ltd., 58 Beaumont Road, Mount Kuring-Gai, NSW 2080, Tel: (2) 457-0011.

GRAND STREET

Editor
Jean Stein

Managing Editor
Deborah Treisman

Art Editor
Walter Hopps

Assistant Editor
Howard Halle

Designer
Jim Hinchee

Editorial Assistant
Julie A. Tate

Administrative Assistant
Lisa Brodus

Interns
Elisa Frohlich
John Henderson
Jeffrey Rotter

Contributing Editors
Hilton Als, Colin de Land, Anne Doran, Morgan Entrekin,
Gary Fisketjon, Raymond Foye, Jonathan Galassi, Stephen Graham,
Barbara Heizer, Dennis Hopper, Andrew Kopkind (1935–1994),
David Kornacker, Jane Kramer, Olivier Nora, Erik Rieselbach,
Edward W. Said, Robert Scheer, Elisabeth Sifton,
Jean Strouse, Jeremy Treglown, Katrina vanden Heuvel,
Gillian Walker, Drenka Willen

Publishers
Jean Stein & Torsten Wiesel

CONTENTS

The Game of Love
and Chance

JÉRÔME SANS: The contemporary world is witnessing a great evolution of the society of leisure. With home shopping and Pay TV, video games and virtual reality, we are developing a full-fledged aesthetics of play.

PAUL VIRILIO: Two attitudes are possible with respect to these new technologies: the first declares them a miracle; the second—mine—recognizes that they are interesting while maintaining a critical attitude. The imminent home installation of domestic simulators and virtual-space rooms for game-playing poses many questions, and in particular this one: "What is a game once the virtual invades reality?"

There are two ways of understanding the notion of play: playing cards, dominoes, checkers; or the play of a mechanical part when it is loose in its housing. I think, in fact, that the second is the angle from which we should envision play today. Play is not something that brings pleasure; on the contrary, it expresses a shift in reality, an unaccustomed mobility with respect to reality. To play today, in a certain sense, means to choose between two realities. A concrete factual reality: meet someone, love that person, make love to that person. Or the game reality: use the technologies of cybersex to meet that person from a distance, without touching or risk of contamination, contact without contact.

What is at play in this case is an illness different from that associated with traditional games and provoked by chance. Gamblers can't do without chance—they are addicted to it and can't break the habit. I believe that alongside those addicted to chance, to roulette, to cards, or to any game, a new kind of addict is being born: the addict of the virtual. People will become hooked on virtuality and will find themselves in an awkward position, torn between two realities. We can already see it on Wall Street and in the stock markets, the casinos where "traders" or "golden boys" play with the virtuality of international markets which are increasingly disconnected from the economic reality of the world.

JS: It's a kind of electronic addiction which leads to a virtual addiction.

PV: You could say that drugs are a game people get "hooked" on. Those who are addicted to card games or the roulette table always end up playing Russian roulette. Games and death, games and accidents, are related. When you play at chance, you are compelled to play and thus no longer free to play; and a physical or mental death occurs. Now video games or the more sophisticated games of tomorrow's virtual reality will induce this same desire for death. A desire to cross the boundary.

I am not a big player. What interests me today in the state of play is cybersex, because it seems to be the most extraordinary aspect of social deregulation. In addition to today's divorce epidemic—which can be attributed to other things than a lack of morality (I'm not playing the moralist here)—another type of divorce is brewing. Instead of living together, people now live apart. An example of this (without cybersex, but in an atmosphere that cybersex will cultivate) is the student couple who invited me to their wedding, and after the ceremony went home separately. They told me, "This way we stay free." "That's great," I said, "your children won't be shocked if you get divorced one day because they'll have divided their time between your two homes anyway."

Cybersex pushes this logic even farther. It's not divorce, it's the disintegration of the couple. You don't make love anymore because it's

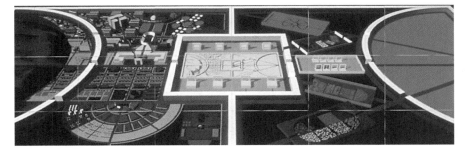

dangerous, because sometimes there are problems—one person may not be very skilled or the situation may get messy. So you use a kind of machine, a machine that transfers physical and sexual contact by waves. What is at play is no longer the connector rod in its housing, but the loss of what is most intimate in our experience of the body.

The actor Louis Jouvet wrote, "Everything is suspect, except the body and its sensations." From now on, with virtuality and electronic copulation, even the body and its sensations will be suspect. In cybersex, one sees, touches, and smells. The only thing one can't do is taste the other's saliva or semen. It's a super-condom.

JS: The sociologist Michel Maffesoli speaks of the development of "neo-tribalism," a desire to regroup, through all the possibilities of long-distance communication. It seems, nonetheless, that we are still dealing with an experience of solitary satisfaction.

PV: I don't believe in a return of tribes and I don't think that a gang is a tribe. As I said in my book *L'Inertie Polaire*, what's on its way is the planet man, the self-sufficient man who, with the help of technology, no longer needs to reach out to others because others come to him. With cybersexuality, he doesn't need to make love at his partner's house, love comes to him instantly, like a fax or a message on the electronic highway. The future lies in cosmic solitude. I picture a weightless individual in a little ergonomic armchair, suspended outside a space capsule, with the earth below and the interstellar void above. A man with his own gravity, who no longer needs a relationship to society, to those around him, and least of all to a family. Maffesoli's tribalization is a totally outmoded vision; the future lies in an unimaginable solitude—of which play is one element.

JS: One has the impression that the player's quest ends in a narcissistic orgasm.

PV: Yes, but it's a narcissism that is expanding.

JS: Some go so far as to say that video games mark a modern triumph of the icon.

PV: Those are the thaumaturgists, the miracle-criers. You have to be extremely wary of what the critic Jacques Ellul called "the technological bluff." Today we have admen, even experts, who spend all their time

saying how wonderful technology is. They are giving it the kiss of death. By being critical I do more for the development of new technologies than by giving in to my illusions and refusing to question technology's negative aspects.

When the railroad was invented, so was derailment. Then there were people like me who said right away that they didn't care if trains were great and went faster than stagecoaches. What was more important was that they not derail, that the accident specific to the train not prevent its development. These people worked on the problems of railroad accidents and invented the "block system" for signalling, which has made the TGV* possible in France. The same can be said for aviation and so on. The accidents of virtual reality, of telecommunications, are infinitely less visible than derailments, but they are potentially just as serious. And there will be no "block system" as long as we listen to the prophets of joy.

JS: Video games have an incredibly imaginative side, a marvelous narrative, a journey through which the player can be transformed into a hero.

PV: This is crucial. In writing societies, the narrative *is* the journey. Melville's first line to *Moby Dick*—"Call me Ishmael"—sets the story in motion, begins Ishmael's journey. In writing, the narrative carries you along. On screen it's the visual rather than descriptive simulation of a voyage (a voyage along tracks, through a labyrinth, through a tunnel),

---

* *Train à Grande Vitesse*, a French express train capable of traveling at over 230 km per hour.

that moves you. Thus the simulator becomes the new novel. And the simulated quality of the virtual journey replaces the poetic quality of the story, whether it be *The Arabian Nights* or *Ulysses*.

JS: So the new player is a traveler.

PV: Yes. But now the travelers are traveled. Dreamers are dreamed. They are no longer free to move about, they are traveled by the program. They are no longer free to dream, they are dreamed by the program.

JS: This player is a hero in a hurry.

PV: He's a man hurried by the machine. Mental images are replaced by mechanical instruments. Reading, one fabricates a mental cinema: each of us sees a different Madame Bovary at her window. In the Bovary video game, there will be only one Madame Bovary, the one in the program.

JS: We're getting back to your old hobbyhorse: the idea that images are weapons.

PV: Cybersex is really the civil war of sex, since people are divided by it. More sophisticated games could replace society altogether. Aren't

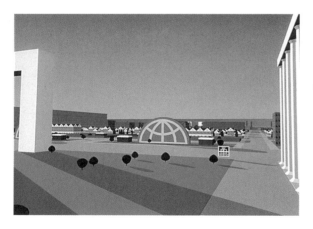

polls—electronic democracy, in a sense—electronic games which are replacing political reality?

JS: What difference is there between video games and the simulations produced by war programs?

PV: As I wrote in *L'Ecran du désert* (my chronicle of the Gulf War), many strategists said that it was easier to understand the Gulf War by buying American video games than by watching the news on television. In a certain sense, they were right. We didn't see concrete events—how the ground troops broke through the Iraqi border, for example—but we did see war transformed into a video game, with the same image repeated over and over: a weapon hitting its target. That image is still very present.

The division of perception into two realities causes a blurring comparable to intoxication: we are seeing double. It's impossible to imagine what this will ultimately produce, several generations down the road. To live in one reality and then, from time to time, enter another, through a night of drinking or hallucinogens, is one thing. But to live all the time through telecommunications and the electronic highway is another. I don't think we can even imagine what it may provoke in people's minds and in society to live constantly with this "stereo-reality." It is absolutely without precedent.

JS: Faced with the plethora of possibilities, what game should we play?

PV: Play at being a critic. Deconstruct the game in order to play with it. Instead of accepting the rules, challenge and modify them. Without the freedom to critique and reconstruct, there is no truly free game: we are addicts and nothing more.

The Laboratories

I.

She takes passage through the grain
Of the sky's electricities. Electric cities.

II.

There is an outer room of stone
And an inner room of foliage
Like a tomb burst with trees.

III.

The somas distilled by the ten bones of the head
Are bright, pleasing, lovely;
The laboratory of the mouth with its nine retorts
Distills bright and innocent saliva,
Dew for her mouth.

IV.

She looks relaxed holding a pair of compasses
Or holding a glass retort.
There is food in sleep.

V.

The demonic tension in the sky means
The master-perfume of the world is forming.

VI.

Lingering in her sheets still
This perfume that is in her sleep is dynamic,
The sheets are white as speeding water.

VII.

She dreams of an exhausted skull
Which rolls out into the sunlight,
Very gently its bones begin to ease
Like the valves of a pinecone
In the warm patch of sunlight
(And a pineal smell expands the forest).

VIII.

And I cannot of course see these dreams
But I can smell their individual stories
In this unfolding scent.

IX.

(A speeding twilight horse the hue of mushrooms.)

The Women Spin

I.

He was a great chemist and studied most in his sea-voyages.

II.

Nude wine all drunk up, bare wine, stripped of its bottle, flesh of wine working all naked within me.

III.

The god in his vaults possessed the child in her womb, speaking in a belly-voice or ventriloquism.

IV.

The altar of the dressing-table where the female sacrament is confected. Prams repainted in tender colors. The kiss over the cradle made them both dizzy. The baby's radiance made them kiss. He was the golden battery.

V.

Standing on the garden path, watching the thunderhulks reflected in the windows of the house, as if the thunder, like a burglar, had broken into the house.

VI.

Silk cocoons shining on the sill like angel-turds of finest silk. The rain water barnacling the windows.

VII.

What does it mean, to say, "The women spin"? They sit there, talking, turning, spinning yarn very slowly—it is their pleasure; then suddenly they reverse and spin fast the opposite way, sending out a strong breeze, like the colored breeze of a musical top.

Reveries

I am magnetized by the mud, the puddled
Windows in it of blue sky,
Its deep filthiness;

Sometimes I cannot take my eyes from it, it is
My reverie. A rain shower flowering
Darkens across the windowsill,

A sweet picklish scent coming from her,
The white reverie or invisible veil of her;
Over this blank

Lipstick and skin-paint and all makeup
Ensure one's relationships, whatever
Behind-the-face feels, she prepares

A meeting-face, the merest lip-twitch
Magnified into winsome smiles in red
And dazzling happy white bone. Mud

Of any color, dark shading, or bright
Brushed-on contours, need give
Nothing but itself, as the sky makes up

At the dressing-table of showers, fixing
The tall flower-masks, the dressing-rooms
Beating with blood, the veils

Throbbing with their power, like
Fountains all around us, she
Turns round and round inside her power,

My star with its strings,
Intelligent tendrils of light
Which squall across their mirrors.

PETER SANTINO

The Pleasure
of Failure

The Pleasure of Failure

Using the fugitive material of sand poured on the floor, Peter Santino attempts to evoke people, places, and times of "personal and national" failure. *My Father's Flag* (1968–1990) is an attenuated triangular sand painting that widens in graded steps to indicate the years between 1968 (the Tet Offensive) and 1990 (the date of the work's installation in New York). The work includes emblematic references to Santino's father, a career soldier elevated here to the rank of Army Colonel (a position he never actually attained), and to Santino's infant daughter. It also uses the Greek letter Omega, the electrical symbol for resistance, to refer to his participation in the War Resisters League. Constant throughout the work is the confrontation and elision of nationalist and religious symbols. Omitting all vowels from the names inscribed in sand, Santino creates a game-like effect for viewers: they are required to crack the code, to search for recognizable names and complete them. They can find, for example, CHRLS MNSN, Charles Manson's name, alongside RCHRD NXN, Richard Nixon; they can reconstruct Mark Rothko or Jackson Pollock. Other names that relate directly to Santino are harder to decipher.

762 Failures (Failure of Communication) (1993), another sand painting, carries a hidden message similar to that of *My Father's Flag*, but is written in Braille script, constructed from molded sand hemispheres. This piece was created at Vienna's Heiligenkreuzerhof exhibition space, in a room that traditionally housed the head of the Dominican Brothers. Although the message is in English, Santino prefers that its content only be guessed at. For another work, *1 Little 1* (1991), Santino constructed twenty squares of sod to function as frames (or backdrops) for the letters he carved out of terra-cotta brick to spell "FUCK DONT MEAN JACK SHIT." This message, meant to travel back in time to the Renaissance, was placed in a small stream, part of the Arno River's watershed, that flows near Santino's former home in Tuscany, and continues on to the Uffizi Gallery in Florence.

If Santino's messages are difficult to decipher or to transmit to their intended recipients, they reflect his concern with "objectifying" failure: seeing failure as an experience to be valued on its own terms. (Santino also directs what he calls the Failure Institute.) The "balls of failure"—a numbered series compressed from materials used in works Santino has had to dismantle—are ultimately a kind of compression, or node, of failure.

—Jackie McAllister

My Father's Flag, 1968–1990

Top and Bottom: *My Father's Flag (Details)*

Top: *762 Failures (Failure of Communication)*, 1993
Bottom: *Detail*

Failure of Left, 1973–1994

Top: *Failure of Left (Detail)*
Left: *(2041) Failure of Son, 1982–1994*
Right: *(2042) Failure of Ghost, 1982–1994*

One Big One, 1991

1 Little 1, 1991

Don't Lick Your Balls: On Golf and Golf Clubs

The following is excerpted from a conversation with Jean Stein, December 1994.

In the movie I've been working on, *Waterworld,* I play a golf fanatic called The Deacon. The movie is set in a water world after the ice caps have melted. But The Deacon knows there's land out there somewhere and he's got to find it because he wants to play golf. First he's going to drill for oil to fuel his jet skis and war machinery. Then he's going to start by building an 18-hole golf course. But he wants to have plenty of land for expansion, 36 holes, 48 holes, 72 holes. He's got some old tapes of Jack Nicklaus, but he's never hit off dry land, he's only hit inside his ship. . . .

So Dwight Yoakam gave me a putter from Tiffany this Christmas. It's sort of a classical putter, the kind that maybe was made a couple hundred years ago. It doesn't have any arrows on it or any kind of clues. And I think it's gold. I hope I can hawk it. But, no, it's a beautiful putter, maybe it could hang on a wall in a bar somewhere. You've really got to know how to putt to use a putter like this; I don't think I'll ever play golf well enough.

I didn't start playing until relatively recently. My father took me out a couple of times when I was a teenager, but I thought it was a sissies' game and I didn't want to be involved in it. A little white ball, a club, hitting it toward a hole. . . it all seemed sophomoric to me and I didn't have any real comprehension of how difficult it was. But when I got sober, I started playing because it gave me something to do.

I first played with Willie Nelson and Coach Royal when I was down in Texas working on *The Texas Chainsaw Massacre II.* We played at Pedernales, Willie's nine-hole course, and he just said, "Keep hitting the ball straight toward the hole until you hear the turkey gobble." You know, he didn't really give lessons. The dress code there was like men could basically wear anything, but they'd prefer them to keep their pants on. Women, they didn't care, but they'd prefer them not to keep their pants on. And when you were out of bounds there, you were really out of bounds—you were in rocks and cactus.

Then I played at a nine-hole executive course out in the Valley in Studio City. I'd see Jack Nicholson driving balls there. Jack probably started playing about the same time as me and he's already shooting in the 70s. I'm just beginning to be able to play in the 90s. This is not great golf. Par on most courses is around 72, and the 70s are where the golf game really is. The greatest thrill in the world is hitting a good golf shot. I know this sounds silly, but it's *incredible*. You're driving 250 yards on a normal shot—two and a half football fields—with precision. And to think that people do that shot after shot after shot...

I took a couple of lessons with Chuck Cook in Austin when I was directing *The Hot Spot*—he's coached the great golfers, Tom Kite and so on. He asked me what club I belonged to and I said, "I don't belong to a club." And he said, "Well, I was going to play with you when I came to L.A. and see how you were doing, but if you don't belong to a club, you'll probably never play golf after you leave here." So I started looking for a club. I tried to join Sherwood. It cost $225,000, and they were only going to take 20 people. They sell the land around the course for houses, and whoever builds a house is guaranteed to get in. So they can renege on your membership any time if they get down to choosing between you and them....You know, any fool who would give them $225,000 just to belong is already crazy. I was one of those people. And they turned me down. I mean, that's ridiculous. That's really sick. Jack Nicholson got in and I didn't. He is charming in the locker room, so I hear. He's a charming guy. He just *might* be a bigger star, and he *might* have a better personality. I think both of those things *may* be true. Those guys still chew tobacco, you know.

Sherwood is where Warner Bros. shot the Sherwood Forest scenes for the original *Robin Hood*. It's in a beautiful area out in Thousand Oaks. By the way, it's the most beautiful clubhouse I've

ever seen in my life. It's like some set for a movie, but they really built the place. The locker rooms are immaculate, and the dining room! It's so well appointed—like Tara in *Gone With the Wind*. It needs Selznick's logo on it. R.J. [Robert] Wagner and Tom Selleck are on the board of directors. They have ranches out there in the Hidden Valley area.

Then there are Hillcrest and the Los Angeles Country Club: one's Jewish and one's Wasp—no Jews, no blacks—but Wasp to the point where they don't take actors either. There's a great story about Victor Mature going to apply at the L. A. Country Club. They said, "We're sorry, Mr. Mature, but we don't accept actors here." And he said, "Actors? Nobody's ever accused me of being an actor before." The club's in that area that goes across Wilshire—it's *half* of Beverly Hills. You don't see any hills in Beverly Hills, because they're all on that golf course.

When the club I eventually got into was hosting the L.A. Open, the other golf courses in L.A. had to be open to its members. So I played at the L.A. Country Club and they *couldn't* not let me. They were cool. Once a year, what the hell. But I heard some funny

stories: Hugh Hefner's place borders on it and he wanted to have a gate opening right onto the golf course from the Playboy Mansion. They nixed that idea real quick. He said, "But I'm going to have bunnies out there on golf carts," and they said, "Like hell you are."

They wouldn't let me into Hillcrest or Brentwood. Then I was trying to get into the Riviera Country Club for years. I was almost accepted, and then it was sold. When I first started applying, it was $28,000 a year for a membership, then it went up to $40,000, then they sold it to the Japanese for $100 million and the Japanese canceled all new memberships. This lasted a couple of years, and everybody kept saying, "Just wait, we'll get through this." Then they started asking me to meetings. When I went up there for my last interview, they said, "Well, watch where you step today, and don't jump around corners because there are a lot of Secret Service men out there. Charlton Heston and Nancy and Ronald are having a little thing out on one of the tennis courts." So, you know, that's the group that's involved. I was finally accepted but it took me five years to get in! They made a mistake, I know they did.

On my first day there, the Malibu fire started, and I was playing with a guy who lived in the Palisades. He looked up and said, "Oh my God, look at that fire! I have to go save my house!" So I played with another guy who couldn't care less whether his house burned down or not. The fire actually started near the Sherwood golf course and that almost burned down too. It was probably a golfer who started it—the last hole went badly for him, and he rubbed a couple of clubs together...

The Riviera is about $75,000, plus $426 a month, whether you play or not. And there are no swimming pool or tennis privileges. There's a locker room where you change your shoes....But it is a George C. Thomas course. It's always in the top fifty courses in the world. It used to be known as Hogan's Alley, after Ben Hogan who won the L.A. Open there in 1948 and '49. The Riviera is a difficult course, the grass is strange and it's hard to hit out of. But it has a history that's hard to compete with and it can't discriminate because it's a course that hosts the P.G.A. tournament.

Before I got into the Riviera, I used to play at Mountain Gate— I call it Mountain Air—up near the new Getty Museum on 405. It's built on a landfill full of Beverly Hills' and Bel Air's trash. You can actually smell the garbage when you're playing, and the greens sort

of fluctuate, you know. And you see things coming up, like a plastic bag. . . . Mountain Air is a very intriguing course; the layout is so strange: it's narrow, there are angles and downhills. You get some very strange lies there—that's what you call it when you hit a ball and it lies at a strange angle. And there are signs that say, "Don't lick your balls." I'm exaggerating, but on certain days the stench is really bad. It's really crowded, and it cost $40,000 when I thought of

joining. I don't know why. It must be very high maintenance keeping that grass green and cut. But they just join like rabbits over there. I don't get it.

Sometimes I play with Neil Young and Bob Dylan above Malibu, on a Japanese-owned public course up in the canyon there. Neil is pretty good. If you learn to play as a child, it comes naturally to you, and Neil has obviously played a lot. His brother was a professional golfer in Canada and his father is a sports writer for the *Toronto Sun*. Bob plays well too. He's sort of taken it up. And Joe Pesci is incredible. I played with him in Venice at the Film Festival when I was President of the Jury and he was there selling *The Public Eye*. And we used to play out in the Valley too. Joe would take me to all these weird courses. I think he is a member of the Bel Air Country Club now. I sometimes play with Dean Stockwell too. He perfected his game at Lakeside when he was doing *Quantum Leap* for Universal. He had a gig that allowed him a lot of time, so he got a beeper and they just beeped him off the golf course. Nicholson says he's even thinking of *building* a golf course during the making of a film. Those are the kind of gigs one looks for these days.

The Stuntman

I was born a stuntman. It's the only kind of work I've ever pursued and I've been in the profession for over thirty years now. I live up in the northeast corner of Utah, in a little town on the Ute reservation called Neola. We used to have a movie come to town once a week, during the war period when I was a youngster. They always showed newsreels—little things about barnstormers, daredevils, and stuff like that. Then there were the various daredevil groups that came around and played in the theaters and at the county fairs in those days—like Jimmy Lynch's Death Dodgers. I guess that may be where I really got motivated by the idea of being a daredevil and taking up that kind of a trade.

I started out when I was a teenager with Orval, "the Daredevil Clown," and we traveled around putting on shows: crashing cars and jumping motorcycles over trucks. Orval had been doing things at the races in Salt Lake, and I was into motorcycle racing and trying to create a career. We kind of joined forces and went on the road with our show, *The Auto Acrobats*. He was a hobo clown and he'd stand on the ramps and let the cars pass by him at a high rate of speed. I was generally dressed in red, white, and blue—our trademark uniform—and I was always the stuntman.

We started out as a strictly daredevil type of thing, but we've gotten into other things over the years. These days we do a lot of car crushing and we're really into big monster trucks. We built one

ourselves that transforms into a robot called Destroyer I. It was featured in a poster magazine. We've now created Generation II: Thundertrax, the transforming 20,000 pound battle tank. We've taken our show throughout the United States. We've jumped cars over anything we could get our hands on—school buses, transport carriers, airplanes flying upside down, and so on. And we do the old two-car head-on collisions. Basically anything we can pick up to go with the show, we'll try.

Back in the old days we saw an act they call the *Coffin of Death*, where a stuntman would blow up the coffin he was lying in. And we came up with the *Russian Dynamite Death Chair* after I picked up a magazine in a motel in Idaho that told how the White Russians would get rid of a political undesirable: they would invite him to dinner and actually blow him up while he was sitting there. I thought that was kind of neat, and wondered how we could recreate it so that someone could actually walk away from it. Then one guy, kind of a drifter, showed up in the early '50s and said, "I know how to do this stunt. I won't do it, but I'll tell you how." He told me what he knew and I thought about it over the years and finally tried it. I lost an eardrum on that one because I didn't have it quite right. So, you know, you learn and sometimes your learning is costly. The next time I got into the chair, I sat back and had a better knowledge of what to do and how to do it. From then on the stunt worked very well.

You sit in a chair with four sticks of real dynamite on the legs and then you ignite it. We use 60-percent dynamite, which is called ditching powder. (The hard-rock miners use a lot of it to blow up what they can't drill.) It's an electric cap, you ignite it with a battery, and you actually blow the chair to bits. You're in the eye of the hurricane. The dynamite blows to the point of least resistance and you need to be in that area of least resistance so that it will blow away from you instead of into you. You have to roll yourself up into a tight ball, in the position you'd take on an airplane if you were about to crash. There are a lot of things that can make a difference: wet ground, if it has been raining, or if the humidity is high. These elements can contribute to the blast and make for a more severe concussion. The dynamite caps are backed up in case one malfunctions. All the dynamite has to go off at the same time or it will blow your arm or leg off. The elements of risk are high.

You ignite it yourself—so that no one else can take the blame for punching the button at the wrong time—and people can see you do it. Then after the explosion when debris is all over the place they can see you there—and they know that you haven't crawled off into the sunset or something. We use a heavy cardboard type of material because wood could splinter and fly into the crowd. We take turns doing the act because after a while the concussion is just so great it will get to you.

You really can't rehearse it. The explosion is so fast: You push the button and either you're there or you're not. We took some video and slowed it way down so we could see the tremendous fireball within the explosion. It'll actually burn you if you're not clothed right or sitting in the right position to protect your face. I wear a hearing aid from doing it. But there's not an insurance company in the world that'll insure a man who's gonna sit on four sticks of dynamite.

From a conversation with Jean Stein.

Cartoon Surrealism

Cartoon Surrealism

CARLO McCORMICK: It seems as if the decadence of Lowbrow, which your art has come to epitomize, had its genesis in the rise of the American leisure class in the 1950s.

ROBERT WILLIAMS: I think you're right. You look back at the '50s as Mr. and Mrs. Idyllic America: the housewife in the apron, the man in the business suit. There were all these standards set up to revolt against, all these ideologies to knock down one by one.

CM: A dominant outlet of youth play in the '50s in which you participated—a seminal landmark in the then-emergent genre of subcultural art—was car culture.

RW: Hot rods were a mechanical-spiritual thing. There were a lot of old cars from the '30s lying around then. People realized that if you took the hood, fenders, and running boards off and put in a new engine, they could outrun any contemporary car. There was a romance to messing with the spirit of the car. There was also a machismo. From car culture, a form of art and graphics developed: pin-striping, flames, scallop paint jobs, metallic and metal flakes, pearlescents, and candy colors. It also involved a sophisticated form of metal craft, welding, grinding, polishing, and chrome-plating. There hadn't been anything like this in the art world before.

CM: The next evolutionary step in this history was the eruption of the Underground Comix scene in the '60s.

RW: Comic book history played a dominant role in my development. In the '50s, there were Senate Subcommittee hearings on the effect of comics on violence and crime. A lot of great comic books fell under the axe at that time, especially the titles from Entertainment Comics. One title that stayed around was *Mad*, later *Mad Magazine*, and its effect was tremendous—on me, Robert Crumb, Rick Griffin, and the rest of American culture. It inspired the kind of humor and sarcasm you found in comedians like Ernie Kovacs and Steve Allen (who were both involved with *Mad* at one time). When all those great comic books disappeared, every kid felt a little revenge, a retaliation, coming on.

It came decades later with the Undergrounds. We did things that not only violated the Comics Code, but violated every code possible,

The Cult Of The Gerning Vishnu, 1994

Explanatory Nomenclature: In As Much As Certain Toothless People Have The Ability To "Gern," Or Smile With Their Bottom Lip Up Over Their Upper Lip Touching Their Nose, The Logical Station For Such Gifted Souls Would Be Benign Deity Or At Least "Holy Keeper Of The Shit-Eating Grin"

Poolroom Title: Swapping "Corner Of The Mouth Jam" With Embarrassing Old Giggling Fartsticks

The Repository Of All Lost Things, 1990

Scholastic Designation: From The Dimension Of Misplaced Things, Evil Harvests What It Wishes Through A Mobius Window And Like The Bo Peep Nursery Rhyme, If We Wait, The Lost Sheep Will Return But In Truth If Bo Peep's Ass Wasn't Attached She Would Lose That Too

Remedial Title: To Donate Is Conscious Intent, To Lose Is Dumb Shit

The Geodesic Specter In The Kaleidoscope, 1991

Scholastic Designation: The Sound Of Rattling Glass Shards In Conjunction With A Vision Of A Cat Killing Figment Of Horror As Imagined By A Pensive Adolescent Who Glares Into A Six-Faceted Dime Kaleidoscope Made In A Distant Land Where Cats Are Generally Eaten

Remedial Title: Besides Sties, Sharing Eye Boogers On A Cardboard Tube-A-Junk Will Give Baby Idiots Pink Eye

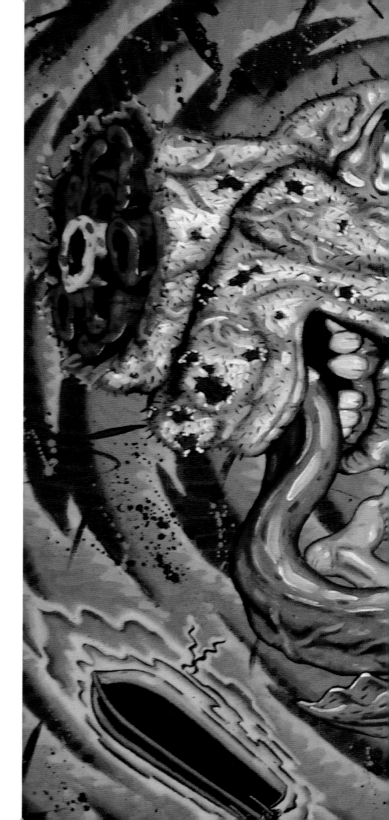

The Face In The Maelstrom, 1988

Museum Catalog Title: A Colossus Squid
Sensory Head With A Dead Man's Hand
Illuminates The Romantic Perils Of a
Pearl Fisher

*Colloquial Title: Aqua Fondling And
The Squid Squat*

A Sandlot Hero Dissipating In The Fast Lane, 1980

Museum Catalog Title: It's Not Winning That's Important But The Way You Masquerade As An Example-Heroica Persona For Young Children Who Would Rather Pass Time Drowning Kittens

Colloquial Title: The Ripe Slugger And The All-Star Snowball

Mr. Man Baby Vs The Strip Mall Boondocks Spoiler, 1994

Explanatory Nomenclature: With An Infantile Hercules An Irony Is Played Out Suggesting A Muscle Bound Baby Future Citizen To Be The Only Foil To Stop A Spined Shopping Center Marauderite From Deforestation, But Who Changes The Diaper Of This Heroic Baby Man?

Poolroom Title: Super Poop Man Regurgitates "The World Is My Nursery"

The Mystic Rabbitmaster, 1989

Museum Catalog Title: The Head Magician Of Luxor Institutes His Personal Hex Whammy Into A Young Hare As He Placates Dame Chance And Encourages Her Fickle Blessing To Insure An Orthodox Set Of Lucky Rabbit's Feet

Colloquial Title: Bunny Ghoul Camel Jockey Carrot Trick

The Voice From The Wee Gee Board, 1990

Scholastic Designation: A Manufacturer Of Parlor Games Ignorantly Produces A Doorway Into The Spirit World Where Naivists Find Their Petty Requests Answered By Being Pulled Through A Ouija Dimension To Become Sexo-Psyche Possessions

Remedial Title: Grease Up The Hole To The Next Dimension Parker Bros., We've Got Another Customer

including laws on pornography. 1963 was just like 1952. The Bohemian movement had advanced some, but the Vietnam War caused such a change. Before then your average kid wanted a high school diploma, maybe a year or two in college, and then a blue collar job. The war stirred an intellectuality, a social consciousness. The white collar ethic developed. No one wanted to get their hands dirty. The buying market became youth-controlled and the youth movement was born.

CM: Your art has graced more than a few rock albums, and you've been known and collected by a slew of bands over the years. How does rock and roll play into this history?

RW: Rock and roll in the '50s wasn't taken seriously at all. The Vietnam War made it very serious. It was no longer a nuisance like comics had been. Then it started getting sweeter, more formal, formulaic, and smooth. Punk was a revolution against that. And a lot of people who were doing punk were also going to art school, so a whole shock wave of art came along with the music. It was like the '50s when Abstract Expressionism accompanied free jazz. Punk art was sloppy with a lot of Day-Glo colors. I was pulled into the energy of that, but I was too much of a draftsman by that point to feel completely comfortable with it. That's when I did my Zombie Mystery Paintings—rough, crude, and fast.

CM: The emergence of new visual languages and art forms is not so much about play as it is about how the playful and serious coexist and interact.

RW: Exactly. Cartoons are a form of mental abstraction, the pictographic language of our time. They have all the earmarks of something that's supposed to be funny, but they aren't necessarily: they can depict tragedy, rape, scenes of extreme vulgarity. You prepare yourself to laugh at something and then it can be heinous. There's a huge middle ground between humor and seriousness, a vast region of abstract thought.

Cartoon graphics have been evolving since the Lascaux caves, Egyptian hieroglyphics, and illuminated manuscripts, and there has been a backlash of people trying to get back to those forms. This is my prediction: people will look at the twentieth century and say rock was the music of the age and comics were the art.

The Day of the Pollyanna

The dough didn't rise that day.
The kitchen clock stopped.
Against all hope
the streetcar turned around
at the Slovany terminal
and started back.

But in the second car,
in the very back, a little girl
wearing a big blue woolen cap
sat holding a doll
that resembled a three-month-old
tapir fetus,
singing, in a tinny voice,

Don't cry...don't cry...don't cry.

Though nobody felt like crying,
tapirs least of all.

Translated from the Czech
by Dana Hábova and David Young

Whale Songs

At two o'clock in the morning
I hear my mitral valve
from the depth of the dim, blood-filled tunnel
which is me. Cellular receptors
fit with a metallic click into the locks
and the cells are me and the locks are me.
From some symphonic distance
there sounds the song of the whales,
and it contains me.

In some black castle
Sleeping Beauty has pricked herself on a thorn,
which is me. The clock has stopped
—in our house, clocks stop at any moment
because she pricks herself at any moment,
on a tiny crock,
on a word,
on a milk tooth,
on a toy that fell into the gutter—
and so there's a still life, *nature morte*,
with me in the genetic background.

A paper kite stiffens in the air,
however, Einstein says, Time is always going, but never gone,
however, my mother says, ten years after her death,
Oh yes, oh yes,
and a clock starts again,
the Invisible passes through the room like a ball of lightning,
Sleeping Beauty lays eggs full of little spiders,
the whales re-enter the tunnel

and I start again
being the machine
for the production
of myself.

Metaphysics

When
he gets leukemia,
he will start a collection of those little coasters
they have in bars, advertising beer,
the largest such collection in the world,
beer coasters for the *Guinness Book of Records*,
by which he achieves some immortality,
the only kind that's really
intelligible.

*Translated from the Czech
by David Young, with the author*

TEXT BY LUIS J. RODRIGUEZ

The Endless
Dream Game of Death

PHOTOGRAPHS BY DONNA De CESARE

Without conscious rituals of loss and renewal, individuals and societies lose the capacity to experience the sorrows and joys that are essential for feeling fully human. Without them life flattens out, and meaning drains from both living and dying. Soon there is a death of meaning and an increase in meaningless death.

Michael Meade (*in his introduction to Mircea Eliade's* Rites and Symbols of Initiation).

We are searching for something, but we don't know what it is. . . At times, we believe we can create a new world.

Maritza, *a member of a Guatemalan mara.**

A boy with dark features stands in a vacant lot near Roosevelt Park in South L.A., wide-eyed, his hair close to the scalp except for a long braid that falls from the top of his head. He wears oversized, neatly-pressed khaki pants and a heavy Pendleton shirt, buttoned to the collar. He is surrounded by five other boys.

For a tense moment, nothing happens. Then one of them strikes him and the action unfurls. Dust saturates the night air. The boy falls. Punches and kicks rain down on him. He tries to strike back, but he doesn't have a chance. After thirty seconds or so—although it seems much longer—Muñeco†, the gang leader or "shot caller," signals for the assault to stop. The others pull back, looking hard at the body, curled in a fetal position in the dirt. One of them helps the youth to his feet. The boys who had attacked him in a violent frenzy now laugh as they shake the battered initiate's hand and embrace him.

"You one of us now," Muñeco says. The boy has joined a smaller clique of the Florencia barrio. The group involved are Cholos, members of a culture that has defined street life in Los Angeles for several generations. "Courting in"—or being jumped by three to eight members for a designated time—is a "sacred" ritual that infers strengthening, painful giving to the group. Other forms of initiation require a proof of the initiate's worth as a "soldier": he may have to challenge

---

*The word *mara* is Central American slang: "I'm going out with *la mara*," someone might say, referring to a group of friends.

†Some of the names in this article have been changed.

a police officer, steal, or stab or shoot someone. Drive-by shootings, in some cases, are simply a proof of nerve.

It has been more than twenty years since I walked the walk and talked the talk of the Cholo, but little seems to have changed. At fifteen I was courted into Las Lomas, a barrio in South San Gabriel, just east of L.A. I got my first tattoo at age twelve. I was eventually arrested several times—for rioting, attempted murder, and assaulting a police officer (I beat all my cases but the last one, which I plea-bargained into two and a half months of county jail time). I shot people. I stabbed people. I fire-bombed homes. I eventually got away from the most violent aspects of "the life," but I never betrayed my barrio.

There is a culture in Los Angeles that consumes. South Central *gangstas* call it being *loc'ed*: crazy enough to act *a la brava**, without caring, to face the bullets as well as to squeeze the trigger or plunge the knife. It's a philosophy against flesh, over flesh, of daring and cleverness and seeming invincibility. In the 1993 film *The Sandlot*, nine prepubescent boys saw baseball not as a game, but as life. The boys played in a junk-strewn lot, without scoring, without winners or losers, just hours of hitting, fielding, throwing, and catching, playing "an endless dream game." Cholos are much the same way. Their power lies in the *being—¡aqui estoy, y que!*[†] But the game that surrounds these outcasts from the dominant as well as the immediate community is death.

From behind the bars of the Heman G. Stark Youth Training School in Chino, a Southern California Youth Authority facility for incarcerated sixteen- to twenty-five-year-old men, members of the primarily Salvadoran gang called Mara Salvatrucha[††] (or MS) discuss their reasons for turning to the gang:

MONO (Raised in the capital of El Salvador, Mono came to the United States twelve years ago. A former drug dealer, he has been a member of MS for seven years.): *We came to Los Angeles from another country without our families, many of whom died in the Civil War. We came*

---

* To do something without hesitation.

† Here I am, and what are you going to do about it!

†† *Salva* stands for Salvadoran, and *trucha*, Spanish for "trout," a fish that swims upstream, symbolizes the fight for survival. *Trucha* in Cholo slang also means "wise" or "alert." MS is considered by police to be one of the most violent of the L.A. street gangs.

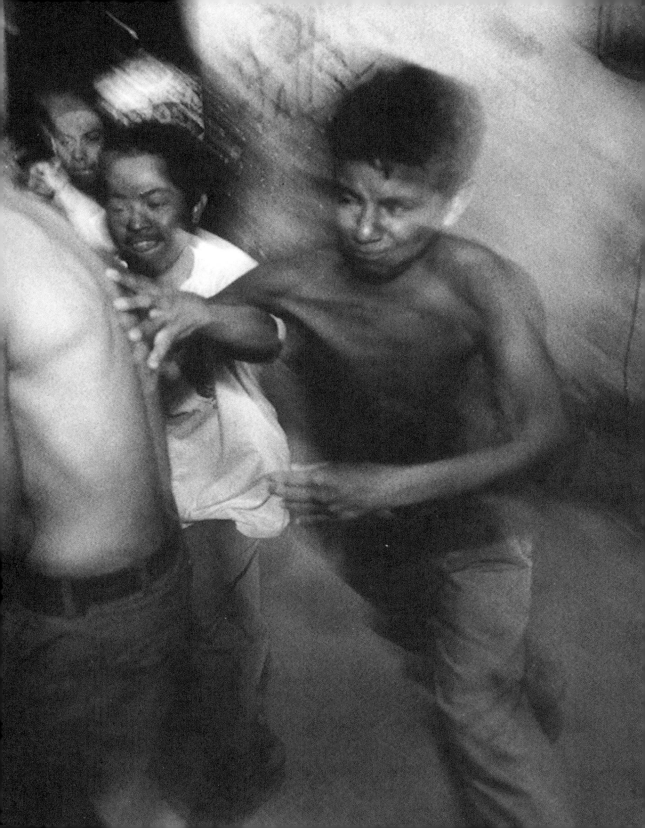

*here for a better life. But we couldn't go anywhere else. . . . So we hooked up
with others just like us. Quickly, Salvadorans united, and we organized
ourselves into MS. We were former military, former guerrillas, former none of
this, and all homeless. That is how it began.*

*I couldn't find work. I didn't have any immigration papers and
couldn't afford to pay rent. At age thirteen, I began selling drugs to survive.
We had to steal just to eat. I didn't come here to ruin this country; I came to
survive. In the MS, I found a form of family. We've come together for our protection. For a name and our people. If you are three times* mojado*,
everyone wants a piece of you.*

*[California governor] Pete Wilson says all Latinos are a weight on the
country. But our women raise their children and clean their houses. The rich
pay Latinos to clean their dogs. In fact, here the dogs eat better than people.
Back home in El Salvador, I had fighting cocks and rabbits. It didn't take
much to take care of them. But here a vaccine for a dog is $100. They have
medical hospitals for dogs, but not for starving children.*

CAPONE (Most of Capone's family was killed in El Salvador. At age
six, he was wounded in the arm. At twelve, he was forced into the military and trained to kill guerrillas.): *I was an orphan and I didn't know
my real father. I saw my adopted father killed. Sometimes it still affects me. I
think about it. I feel rage. Only my adopted mother and two brothers survived.*

*I have nothing but love for MS: for Salvadorans, but also for the barrio.
We are for each other. For the tradition, even if we fight each other.*

PATO (He left school in El Salvador after the first grade to become
a farm worker and later came to the U.S., hoping to get an education.
One night in Hollywood, he was beaten with an iron bar by gang
members. Soon after, he joined MS.): *It was ugly where I was in El
Salvador. I left for the fields early in the morning, and by the time I came back,
many people would be killed. Children in the village were being trained for
the army from nine years old on; their bosses were older, eighteen to twenty-five.
You had little kids holding M-16s. The guerrillas, they had their babies
born into war. The children didn't know anything else. At age ten, they were
already dangerous.*

*The young dudes here keep the war going. They do drive-bys at thirteen.
When I get out, I want to work like a normal human being. I don't want any*

---

*An undocumented immigrant or "wet one." Salvadorans have to cross three
  borders (Guatemala, Mexico, and the U.S.) to reach Los Angeles.

more prison. What good is selling drugs? What good are robberies? Being in jail all the time? I have learned: my first crime will be my only crime.

Between 1910 and 1920, the Mexican Revolution and related political turmoil caused more than a million people to cross into the U.S. Attracted by the glut of jobs tied to rail and industrial development and welcomed for their willingness to work for low pay, many of them settled in the ravines and hills throughout L.A. County where labor camps were constructed. These areas with their minimal housing—usually without sewers, paved streets, or plumbing—became the first barrios.

Faced with widespread discrimination and social ruptures, the immigrants began to forge an identity of resistance. Barrio gangs emerged in the 1930s among the children of the first wave, influenced by the culture which had arrived with migrant workers from El Paso, Texas. Within ten years, these "Pachuco" street corner societies, made up of estranged collectives of adolescents in rebellion against the police and the customs and mores of parents and teachers, had integrated African American music and dance into their own culture. The zoot suits of eastern ghettos and gangster movies such as *The Public Enemy*, combined with underworld speech from Mexico and the border region, helped to create a completely new American persona. The epitome of cool, or *suave*, the Pachucos wore finger-tipped coats, long, baggy pants pulled in at the ankles, large feathered hats, suspenders, and pocket chains and talked their own slang, or *calo*.

Cultural difference had its price, and the local media, along with police departments and other official agencies, began a campaign of terror against these "zooted hoodlums." Incendiary articles and headlines appeared in the *Los Angeles Times* and the *Los Angeles Herald & Express*: "Web of Zoot Suit Gangs Spread Over Entire L.A. Area," "Homes Invaded in Hunt for Pachucos," or "Boy-Gang Terror Wave." All of this culminated in the infamous Zoot Suit Riots. U.S. Marines and sailors stationed in and around Los Angeles were itching for a fight before going to war overseas. The press-fueled animosity toward Pachucos during the Sleepy Lagoon Trial led to the murder conviction of twelve Mexican boys in January of 1943. In turn, Pachucos beat and robbed sailors who landed in Mexican neighborhoods. The Chavez Ravine Naval Base, at the heart of the

Los Angeles, 1993.
"Baby Bugsy" and "Little Crime" peewee Salvatruchas hanging out at one a.m. on the street corner where the Mara Salvatrucha gang was founded.

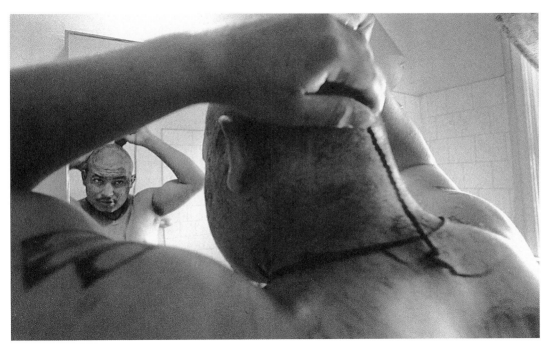

Los Angeles, 1993.
"Pato" shaves his head in a style popular with the 18th Street gang. He leaves a "homeboy braid" at the back.

Palos Verdes barrio, reported several trainees who were taunted and sometimes attacked and "rolled" by Mexican youth. These actual and rumored attacks added to the sailors' violence. Police responded by waiting until the servicemen had beaten or stripped several youths—then they arrested the victims.

Pachucos and Mexicans returned from overseas duty (having garnered more medals than any other ethnic group) to increased discrimination. And widespread introduction of heroin to the Los Angeles area created the first of many generations of *tecatos* and *pintos**. Pachucos evolved into Cholos, who sported oversized military and correctional facility clothing, shortened hair, bandannas, and skull caps. In the '60s, national law enforcement programs, such as COINTELPRO—which infiltrated and helped to dismantle the Black Panthers, the Young Lords, and much of the American Indian Movement—destroyed or weakened many of the existing Chicano organizations. David Sanchez, former head of the Chicano paramilitary group, the Brown Berets, claims that he disbanded it because there were so many government infiltrators he didn't know whom to trust. At least two other Chicano activists died in what were believed to have been "political hits." Barrio warfare flared up in earnest, helped along by an influx of firearms from returning Vietnam vets and more drugs, such as PCP and cocaine. The first major drive-bys were documented at this time.

The subsequent closing of local factories and plants, such as Bethlehem Steel, American National Can, and Uniroyal, left many Los Angeles residents desperate for work. And by the 1980s, a new wave of immigrants, including Central Americans fleeing upheaval in their homelands, led to the creation of new gangs such as Mara Salvatrucha.†

Police agencies in the Los Angeles area instituted several efforts to suppress gang membership and generated computer files on about half of the teenage male population—close to 50,000 young men— in South Central L.A. Police reportedly began using the letters NHI (No Human Involved) to designate gang members who have been

---

* Heroin addicts and those who have done prison time.

† By 1989, law enforcement officials acknowledged 770 gangs in the Los Angeles metropolitan area, with Latino gangs accounting for 60 percent of the total, and of the more than 800 gang-related deaths in L.A. County in 1992, about 70 percent involved Latino gang youth.

shot or killed. The rebellion in April 1992, following the acquittal of the police officers charged with beating Rodney King, brought national attention to the organized street gangs involved. Shortly afterward, the U.S. Immigration and Naturalization Service's Violent Gang Task Force began targeting alleged undocumented gang members for deportation.*

One breezy summer evening in 1993, the Frances Street Locos, a subgroup or clique of the Mara Salvatrucha gang, called for a special meeting in Koreatown[†] to discuss a mandated effort to end random drive-by shootings in Los Angeles barrios—a decree initiated by the oldest prison group in California, *La Eme*, the Mexican mafia founded in the 1950s by Los Angeles inmates.

At 6:30—soon after dusk—several homeboys began walking toward the meeting place; one dude in a black hood directed the others, two at a time, to an apartment complex. They were cautious, aware that they had enemies in the surrounding streets. They entered the elevator of a three-story stucco building, inhabited by Salvadoran immigrants. Dance rhythms blared from windows; TV lights sprayed a room; the smell of *pupusas*[††] wafted by; elaborately stylized MS graffiti decorated steps and doorways and culminated in one large memorial piece: R.I.P. Indio (a deceased homeboy's barrio name).

In the tiny but well-kept apartment, gang members between the ages of thirteen and eighteen—Clever, Triste, Scoobie, Boxer, Rascal, and Psycho, among others—sat around on a carpeted floor. They were wearing size-50 pants, held up with thin belts, some cut off below the knee, with ironed white T-shirts. Most were tattooed *pinto* style: on hands, arms, fingers, below the eyes, on foreheads, napes, thighs, behind one boy's ear. Many bore the three triangular-shaped dots signifying *Mi Vida Loca* or had their barrio-gang name emblazoned on their backs or stomachs. One member had a tattoo across

---

* As of January 1995, the Gang Task Force had deported more than 780 gang members.

† Koreatown is home to one of some fifteen Mara Salvatrucha cliques in and around Los Angeles, in the communities of South Central, Hollywood, Huntington Park, and the San Fernando Valley. But its fastest-growing cliques are actually in El Salvador, due to deportations or voluntary removal. Many of the Cholo rituals, symbols, and codes now appear throughout El Salvador.

†† A Salvadoran food staple, made with fried cornmeal and stuffed with meat, cheese, and salsa.

Los Angeles, 1993.
"Trigger" is fifteen. He lives at this Mara Salvatrucha crash pad with ten other youths.

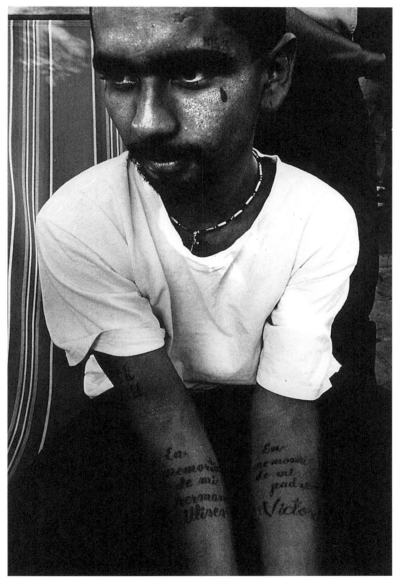

El Salvador, 1994.
Victor Diaz's tattoos recount the death of his brother in the Los Angeles
gang wars and the murder of his father by Salvadoran government soldiers.

his chest that read: *Perdon mamacita mia, por mi vida loca* (Forgive me, my dear mother, for my crazy life). Others had jail scenes, sayings such as *Smile Now, Cry Later*, skulls with sombreros, spiders in webs (sometimes to cover needle marks on the inner arm), epitaphs, names of girlfriends or favorite songs. The music, though it now included hip hop, still focused on the "oldies" and L.A.–style sounds: the "Huggy Boy" collections, *18 With a Bullet, The Town I Live In*, and *Have I Sinned?*

In less than fifteen minutes the meeting was declared over. The participants had agreed to send a representative to the larger meetings between *La Eme* and the L.A. barrios.

"This is how we're going to keep the peace," Clever said. "From now on, we're going to defend each other, one on one. Or two on two. If somebody wants to shoot someone, they have to get out of the car and walk up to the person they're going to shoot. And if someone brings out a gun, it better be to use it. If you don't plan to use it, don't bring it out."

"Before, they'd shoot wildly into a group," said Scoobie. "Most of the time they don't hit nobody but a woman or some child."

Now, a year and a half since the decree went into effect, drive-by casualties have decreased considerably.* The number of gang-related murders in L.A. county has also dropped significantly over the last two years.

"What the police, social agencies, and gang-prevention programs couldn't do, the dudes in the joint did," a former *pinto* tells me with pride. Veteran barrio leaders from the prisons have also been instrumental in establishing calmer communication among several communities. By mid-1994, Latinos and African Americans in Venice and Latinos and Asians in Long Beach had found some tenuous form of peace. Not all the barrios, particularly those on L.A.'s vast east side, have been cooperating. Those who don't abide are subject to "green lights"—condoned attack by other barrios in the streets and in correctional facilities around the country. And there are, as Clever says, "green lights everywhere." The decree has also allowed another aspect of street life to flourish: drug sales, a means of short-term survival for many.

*According to one account, incidents have fallen by 70 percent in the San Fernando Valley alone.

"Any peace is undermined unless it is linked to a viable future," says Ruben Guevara, an artist who works with gang youths in East L.A. "I mean decent employment and meeting the educational and social needs of Latino youth." Seventeen-year-old MS member Bosco adds, "There's not much action since the peace started. There's nothing to do, no work, no place to go."

The peace efforts have also been jeopardized by new fears. During the two months between the beginning of last fall's school semester and the November 8 elections, thousands of primarily Latino youth, gang and non-gang members, carrying Mexican and Central American flags, repeatedly left their schools and took to the streets to protest the statewide "Save Our State" initiative.* On October 16, some 100,000 people gathered in front of City Hall in downtown L.A. for what is said to have been the largest demonstration in the city's history. By October 28, the police had placed the city on tactical alert. Proposition 187 passed with 59 percent of the vote statewide.

Soon after the elections, Lupe, a second-generation resident of South Gate, complained of having been harassed at a mall by Anglos calling her a "wetback." "I've had racist remarks before, but this was out there," she said. "I know it was because of Proposition 187." Although most MS members are immigrants, the vast majority, like myself, came to this country as children between the ages of one and five. Some have residency papers or are citizens by virtue of birth. Most came here to work and are not on welfare. Yet, as one member said, "even though I got my papers, there are still people who think I'm illegal. It doesn't matter to them. We're all brown, and we're all no good."

Unfortunately, members of this second generation are often without work. Some of them even blame the undocumented immigrants for the lack of jobs in the community rather than directing their anger at the large industries that have abandoned the city. In their absence, the main manufacturing opportunities in L.A. are in nonunionized sweatshops that draw on a vast pool of recently immigrated labor. These outposts of the L.A. garment industry often evade the $4.25 minimum wage requirement by paying per piece. Workers generally

---

* Proposition 187 denies educational, nonemergency health care, and social services to undocumented immigrants. It also requires doctors, school teachers, and principals, as well as public officials, to report any suspected undocumented immigrants.

Los Angeles, 1994.
Immigration police arrest suspected gang members for loitering without documents.

Los Angeles, 1994.
A sign protests against U.S. social policies and Proposition 187.

work long hours and are not eligible for workers' compensation. "I can't get a job," complained one Chicano gang member living at the Estrada Courts Housing Developments in East L.A., "but some guy just over the border can." The unemployed gang members, targeted for deportation, are often sent to places they no longer know or never knew. A deported MS member, now serving time in El Salvador, tells how Salvadoran police burned his "homeboy" braid and beat him for being a "tattooed Cholo."

SANTOS (An MS member who served five years at the Youth Training School for attempted murder. He earned a high school diploma and an Associate of Arts degree there. He is currently unemployed, living in El Salvador with his sick grandmother.): *The police went after me because they said I looked like the one who did it. I didn't do it but it was their word against mine. I resigned myself to the prison. I did good there. I didn't want to hang around the gangs. I wanted to be on my own. When I got out after five years, I felt my whole life was before me. Then Immigration came to deport me. I tried to fight it. I spent another year in the federal jail for immigrants in downtown L.A. I had lawyers. I had letters of support from my teachers. But I lost hope. I know I shouldn't have. But it got so hard just waiting behind bars. I got deported.*

Mathematician

Dismembered figures taking form from the page they were calculated on. The unending geometry of his salvation. Body counts that rise as he holds the wrong belief. Or uses the product of a manufacturer who does not obey the Ten Commandments. Small open graves reflected in his spoon. Causing him to rise from his seat. Causing him to say, "May the slaughtered sheep of my kingdom come forth and be redeemed. May their redemption be measured in complimentary sets of silverware." For he wanders through the streets calling out his own name. For someone has subtracted him from a calculation he will never see. For he approaches a woman who viciously denies that her breasts are billowing zeppelins, that her eyes. They are so blue.

Divining

God finally destroys the devil and accidentally disappears. I steal the bread of understanding and cast it to the duck pond. I have done what is good until an old and wise mallard looks me coldly in the eye, whispers that I have caused overpopulation, eventual starvation. It occurs to me that I give to charity only so calf-eyed children can continue to lead quiet lives. The urge to go on a three-state killing spree. Or help an old woman to cross the street. The realization that any action has an equal and opposite reaction, that to do any one thing is to kill the other. Parts of my body crawl away and are never seen again. I win friends. Their limbs fold back into a tree that leaves no seed. A tree that begs me to eat its red fruit. A tree that tells me the road to hell is paved with ordinary asphalt.

A Translation, Purdy Group Home

Know that girl in the green sweater?
He ate her.
Had chicken in his mouth
then only a bone.
They say it's lions' heads he keeps in his refrigerator—
it's people.

I die easily in here.
I need help for my hands.
Showers kill easily.
My head spins around at times.
I notice that I am about to stand
and through God (with hatred enough at times)
I am killed over and over again.
I am standing in the place and the place changes.
I am the changing of the place.

Sunlight Floods the Room. Three Are Drowned.

I am out of sight
I am out of mind
I sadly fear my mittens
I am lost

The sign says—DON'T WALK
I crawl across the street
The secrets I think of
Begin to think of me

I am the man on the window ledge
Who jumps out the window for some air
I am not an actor
But I play one on TV

I feed the hand that bites me,
feed gravy-soaked sponges to every dog
I have created God in my own image
He approves of this

CHRISTIAN SCHUMANN

The Origami Knight

Some time in early August of 1900, the map of the Antipodes made its first public appearance at one of the Uyterhoevens' afternoon teas, on the dictionary stand in the library. It was made of goatskin and cotton cloth, cross-hatched in a checkerboard design—it looked to be a chessboard, in fact—except that some-one had drawn the outline of what was very clearly a landmass across the top, a shape that some of the more frequent guests at the "chess garden" compared to a ghost in flight and others to a windblown star.

The doctor claimed to have found the map in the games shack at the back of the property. He said that he'd been cleaning out the dresser there—which many considered the least credible part of the story—and that he'd found it folded up behind a panel in one of the top drawers. From there he'd taken it straight to the library and set it in the dictionary's anointed place for all the guests to see. He even moved the terrestrial globe over to stand beside it, in hopes that someone might be able to find a shape somewhere on the globe to match the one on the map.

The doctor himself claimed to have had no luck. He'd suspected that the seams of the cross-hatch design might represent lines of longitude or latitude, but they hadn't been marked, and there was no ledger either, so it wasn't even clear how big the place was, whether it was continent- or more island-sized. Judging from the topology, by what appeared to be several anonymous rivers and a mountain range across the southern part, the dimensions looked to be somewhere in between. Aside from that, however, there'd been very little else to go on—just the shape and the name, which had been written in thin capital letters, in an arc across the face: T-H-E A-N-T-I-P-O-D-E-S.

The doctor gave the guests several weeks to ponder the question, but by the last days of August, still no one had found a suitable match anywhere on any of the doctor's globes or maps, and a consensus was reached that these Antipodes must therefore be uncharted—other, of course, than by the negligent author of this mysterious map.

That settled, questions of greater weight had come in greater number: if the Antipodes were, in fact, unknown, what was life like there? What were the animals like? What were the trees and plants and people like, if there even were people? Numerous different parties of children had discussed the matter over lemonade at the garden. In particular, they'd wondered what sort of games the native Antipodeans might play, whether they were at all like chess or checkers—as the map itself had seemed to suggest—or whether their games had different rules altogether.

Of course, the only way to know for certain was to find the Antipodes, and the only way to do that—in the absence of any geodetic assistance—was to go look. So that was why the doctor was supposed to have left. He was going to search for the Antipodes. He insisted on going alone, because he wanted to travel light, but he said that he would be taking a chess set with him as well, so that in the event he did find the place pictured on the map, he would have something to offer the natives as a gift, in return for which he hoped they might offer him a game of theirs that he could send back to the garden, along with whatever explanation of the rules he had been able to glean. So armed and so determined, the doctor left on September 3rd, bound for the opposite side of the world.

•

October 24, 1900
Dear Sonja,

How is one to know, I wonder, if a backgammon counter is sleeping or if it is only resting? If it is dreaming or daydreaming, and what of its dreams—what must they contain? Beside me lies the answer—polished red, round, and perfectly still—a young counter and my newest friend.

Still, I haven't the faintest idea if it is napping now, or listening in as I compose my thoughts for you.

There is so much here to understand. It's one of the reasons I've been slow to write. I haven't wanted to commit any of my impressions to words, for fear that I might round the next bend and find something there which overturns everything I'd thought I understood. For this is a more astonishing place than any of us anticipated—more astonishing by far. The Antipodes are indeed a land of games, strewn with every different kind of piece one can imagine, looking much the same as normal pieces do, except that here they all have life, are of life-size, and move and will and think.

But even as strange as this may be, it is also my observation that once one has come to accept this single local convention—that one's company is comprised entirely of pieces—the rest all seems to follow naturally thereof. The rules of society and conduct all make perfect—I am even tempted to say common—sense. Is it not common sense that darts should fly through the air alongside sparrows, that black fields of clover should shine beneath the sun like tar? That checkers stack, that backgammon counters roll, that dice tumble, that playing cards travel in hands or packs, and that cribbage pegs scissor down the street like stilts?

It is all, that is to say, very much as you would imagine, and the same holds true of one's impressions. I mean that my opinions of the various pieces here are the same as they have always been. The dice I observe to be arbitrary creatures. They tumble wherever they like, guided by no particular purpose; not the sort upon whom I'd stake much value or place much trust. The marbles are sleek and knowing. The playing cards are bullies, swindlers, and bluffers who, as I understand, generally inhabit the southern province of Katalin, which for that reason I shall be trying to avoid.

I have tended, as you might guess, to gravitate toward the chess pieces, who are as ever an exceedingly trustworthy ilk, duty-bound, forthright, guided by reason that I recognize and discernible calculation. And yet it isn't only this that brings me so often in their company. There is also the fact that among the chess pieces—and only the chess pieces—are what are here called "effigy" or "representational," as opposed to "totem" or "abstracts"—a fairly essential distinction to keep in mind.

When I say "effigy," I refer to those pieces that look like something other than just a game piece. Thus far, I have come across effigy of elephants, scythed chariots, Asian foot soldiers, castles, towers, jesters, runners, buccaneers, troubadours, and Roman soldiers, all of whom resemble their likeness not just in appearance but in behavior as well. Again perfectly reasonable, but of inestimable comfort to me, since I cannot deny, particularly as I find myself in such an unfamiliar place, that I do derive a certain amount of reassurance from being among those who, despite the plumage of their costumes or the exaggeration of their features, do at least resemble me in species. So let me simply admit that though the landscape belongs to pieces of a seemingly infinite variety, it is the map of the most civilized effigy (by which I simply mean those which most resemble man) which I have been touring, their society in which I have tended to circulate, their place-names I use; it is their world, in other words, that I have entered into.

But now let it be clear that though the effigy have predominated my experience, they are nonetheless very much in the minority here, the majority of pieces being "totem," which denotes the fact that they do *not* appear to be anything other than what they are. Totem simply are what they are. Dice are totem, then. Dominoes are totem. I am told that marbles are the most ancient of totem. Checkers are totem, and many chess pieces are totem as well, as you yourselves can attest. A Staunton pawn, for instance, does not appear to be anything other than a pawn (aside perhaps from a bedpost), so it is regarded as a totem as well.

Of course, it is precisely this selfsame quality of the totem which has hampered my getting to know them better. I simply don't feel that I have much in common with them, at least as compared to the effigy. Totem have no eyes, after all (with the exception of the chess knights, who almost all look like horse busts, officially qualifying them, I should think, as effigy, and yet I don't believe they are), likewise (with the exception of the knights) none of the totem has a mouth to speak with, or ears to hear, or a nose to smell with. I assume they can touch and feel, since they can move, but that seems very little on which to forge real sympathy or communication. So, notwithstanding the perceptible influence which they can exert on a room—and the chess totem in particular have a way of making one feel slightly crude and foolish—most of the totem remain fundamentally enigmatic and inscrutable to me, which may help explain why it was not until yesterday that I truly befriended my first, and was rewarded by the extraordinary events which have finally compelled my pen back to paper.

Specifically, I had been making my way along a road called Triboli when a red backgammon counter came up from behind to join me. To the naked eye, it may have seemed an indistinct piece—a flat red marble wheel is all—but such are the limitations of the naked eye, for my more intuitive appraisal of this counter was of an individual every bit as distinct and idiosyncratic as any piece or person that I have come across, of an open, playful, and generous nature which I would also contend, if asked, was youthful.

Naturally, being a disk, the counter was more swift than I, and so as we became acquainted, it tended to roll all about the road, tracing figure eights and twisting wreaths; it would circle back behind me and then race ahead, and was even able, if I lengthened my step and slowed my gait, to slip between my legs.

So we made our way, without much mind of time or destination, until at a certain spot along the way, marked by no sign or fork that I could see, the counter rolled off the road into the ditch and stopped. I stopped as well, thinking that perhaps my friend had lost its way. I waited for it to climb back up, but it remained. I beckoned to it to return. I actually called to it as if it might hear, but it answered by turning two more rotations away from the road, then stopping again—waiting, it seemed, for me.

Well, among the greatest pleasures of being here, I find, is that I've no appointments to keep. So we traveled into the countryside, I the happy subject of what seemed to be the counter's whim, and soon found ourselves in an orchard of lemon trees and another tree whose fruit I would compare to certain descriptions I have read of the avocado. On we ventured so far and long that even our shadows began to stretch and yawn for evening, until finally we came in view of one particular tree, so distinctive and arresting I knew when I saw it that we'd come to our destination.

It rose up three lengths higher than those surrounding and was the size and shape of an oak; at first glance, as fine a tree for climbing as one could hope to find, with strong outstretched limbs shrouded everywhere by leaves which were thick and dark and waxy like magnolias. But as I came closer, I could see what made this tree so magnificent was neither its foliation nor its physique, but its blooms, which were not flowers, nor fruits, but candles; candles everywhere throughout its crown, on every limb and elbow, high and low; candles, all ivory-colored and standing up the length of human hands, each one slightly tilted to its own attitude but yielding a straighter line of hardened candle drip beneath, traced on every leaf or twig which interrupted the descent of its melted wax; everywhere the stalks hung down like icicles, and as we passed through the last of the orchard trees, I saw that down beneath them, all across the moss and twisted roots that surrounded the base, were hundreds upon hundreds of amber drip castles—an entire kingdom there, rising up no higher than my hip and comprised entirely of candle drips, the color and translucence of honey, layer upon hardened layer, each applied with such whim and patience I recognized the hand of nature and not of man.

I wanted to go to see them and walk among them, but I wasn't sure I should. The red counter had stopped just outside the edge of this golden kingdom, and a certain boundary was suggested by a ring of seven stone benches which encircled the umbrage, save for where a small creek ran along the side farthest from us.

I looked back at my friend to see if it might give some indication whether I was free to invade this perimeter, but there beside him now was another counter, and two more a bit farther around—one green, one white, one brown. They'd come up through the orchard and taken their places alongside my friend with an equally meditative aspect. I thought perhaps I should do the same. I took a seat on one of the stone benches, and as darkness descended, I watched as more and more counters emerged from the landscape. I could just barely see them rolling in from the trees, shadows floating up the creek and tumbling up the banks, and all dutifully taking their places round the tree. They seemed to be waiting, though I'd still no sense what for, until—out of thin air— a candle on the nearest bough above me lit. Then another on the far side did the same, and then another, and another. And as more of the counters settled in their positions, more of the candles began to light. One by one the little flames ascended higher and higher up the boughs, their excitation here and there declared by the scamper of squirrels, or the chirp and brief round flight of birds who made their nests near by.

As I sat watching this luminous twilight bloom ascend the tree, I was suddenly startled by a movement in the boughs, of something larger than a bird or a squirrel rushing up through the branches. I couldn't see it well, it moved so quickly, but it was dark and very agile, and much larger in size than its lightness on the boughs would have suggested. It looked almost human, sitting there quietly like an Indian. I was close to calling up when just then the flicker of several more candles drove it even higher. It climbed as high as the tree would allow, and stopped just barely in my sight.

All the candles appeared to have lighted now, and darkness had descended about most of the sky. I wondered if this creature might be trapped there all night, but just as I stood to call up, I was stopped short again by the entrance of another character. It quite startled me, in fact, as I'd not heard it coming. It entered from the orchard, through the circle of counters—a figure all in white, with white face and hands; a knight, I recognized, of human build and proportion, but for some difference which I couldn't yet discern, he was moving so swiftly.

He made his way straight to the trunk, and looked up into the boughs with something of a craftsman's purpose, intending to climb, and apparently unaware that anyone was watching. Like a squirrel, then, and just as fast, he scrambled up the bark and out upon the lowest limb, lengthwise peering at the nearest candle. The branch strained not at all beneath him, even as he reached out to coax the candle from its cup. Something was very strange about this fellow, something strange and marvelous, but I couldn't tell what it was until he'd plucked the candle from its stem and raised the burning wick up near his face.

He blew gently at the flame, teasing it to flicker, but I could see his features by its golden light, so creased and straight, so flat and smooth: he was made of paper, folded of a single sheet, like rice or tracing paper—an origami knight. He reached to coax a second cup and candle from their place, and I could see better—a more exquisite creature never was, in gesture as well as feature. Every move he made, the turn of his wrist or tilt of his neck, was perfectly enunciated by the flex of some tiny crease or fold. And so I watched in awe as now, with candles in each hand and all the grace of one who has no weight to sprain his landing, he dropped from the bough like a leaf.

Without a moment's pause, he then crossed to one of the drip-castles nearby me, and began melting the wax with his flames. And I understood, not even so much from his actions as from his manner, that something must be hidden inside. He worked anxiously, several times looking over his shoulder as he passed the small flames over the yielding surface. Twice he looked in my direction, but apparently from within the glare of the candletree he could not see out.

Nor did he see, up in the tree itself, the shadowed figure that was lurking there. It had descended from its perch. In fact, from the moment of the knight's appearance, it had been crawling down branch by branch, and had now paused midway, peering through the leaves and candles at him.

I could see it better now. It was distinctly the shape of a man, and he had something long and thin in his hand. I wasn't sure what it was, but then he pulled something from over his shoulder—a long tinder—and I suddenly became alarmed, for as he reached out to light its end by the nearest candle, in the sudden flare of light I could see this was an arrow in his hand, and that he had a bow as well.

I couldn't think what I should do, whether I should stand and make my presence known, but at just that moment, just as this strange figure stretched his arrow against the bow and trained its fiery tip upon the hunched back of the unsuspecting knight below, a sudden gust swept through the orchard. There was a mad thrashing in the boughs as a flaming arrow came whistling through the leaves and spiked the castle next to the white paper knight, who turned just in time to see the dark assassin come tripping down the branches like an ornament falling from a Christmas tree. He struck the ground like a kernel of popped corn, and—I could see very clearly now—he was precisely like the white knight, made all of paper, but the sheet from which he'd been folded was the color of coal.

He scrambled to his feet in an instant, drew a second arrow from his quiver, and lit it by the nearest candle in the boughs. Slowly then he turned to address his white opponent, who was standing before his melted castle now, holding his candles out like two stilettos.

"Timothy."

"Odin," replied the white knight.

The black knight—Odin—pointed to the melted castle with his flaming arrow, and his voice was thick and dry, like whispers. "What is inside?"

Timothy stepped back for him to see—as yet only a simple wooden handle was exposed. Odin, the black knight, gestured for Timothy to continue, so Timothy knelt down again and applied his two flames to the wax. Slowly it began to melt away. Odin stepped closer to see, and suddenly Timothy flung one of his candles at him. Odin dodged it easily and, unoffended, bowed. "Now take it out," he said. Timothy, unashamed, obliged. He took the handle and pulled it from the syrupy wax.

I could not see what it was at first, but as Timothy ran the flame of his remaining candle along its edge, the shape came clear: it was a hand mirror.

Odin held out his hand. "Give it to me."

Timothy shook his head.

"It's no use," Odin extended the tip of his burning arrow, but Timothy only began to circle slowly. He held the mirror behind his back and I could see how heavily it hung from his delicate paper hands.

Odin did not wait. He swept his flaming arrow at Timothy like a swordsman, but the white knight jumped and tumbled toward the tree trunk, mirror still in hand. Odin lunged again, and this time caught Timothy's hand. The flame licked up to his arm before he rolled behind the trunk and frantically beat his limb against the ground to put it out.

Odin spoke as if to the tree, which stood between them now. "I don't mean you harm. Just leave the mirror there." Timothy did not move. "I'll tell no one you were here. I'll tell them I found it, and I'll show them where." Odin waited, but Timothy's reply came not in words. With his one good arm, he tossed the mirror up into the air, then scrambled up the trunk to catch it upon the first limb.

Odin looked up at him with both pity and admiration. "You are a fool," he said, but Timothy only crept farther out along the limb, the mirror now swinging pendulously from his good hand.

Odin began to laugh, but then without warning leaped up with his arrow still aflame. Quick as a flash, Timothy scrambled up to the second branch, and again they stared at each other, for a moment perfectly still.

"Very well," said Odin, and which of them moved next, I cannot say, the other answered so quickly. Like lightning they bolted from their places and raced through the candletree after each other, faster than the light from Odin's arrow could follow. Birds flew squawking from their nests. Whole stalks of wax came falling down onto the castles below, but neither knight ever teetered or was unsure. For the briefest moments they would pause to taunt each other, poised on the very fingertips of boughs. Then they'd dash up or down while all the burning wicks yearned after them.

Then, three quarters of the way up the tree, all stopped. A last candle stalk fell and broke softly on the moss, and this time it seemed that Odin had finally won. He'd chased Timothy out onto a high branch from which there appeared to be no escape. Timothy's chest was heaving from the burden of the mirror, but he had one last plan in mind. Very deliberately he took one more step. The branch bowed heavily.

"What are you doing?" asked Odin. Timothy held the mirror out into the darkness as far as he could, gripping it by the fingertips of his one good hand. "Don't!" came Odin's cry, but Timothy only looked back at him, nodded, and then tossed the mirror high up into the darkness.

Before it left Timothy's hand, Odin had already dropped his arrow and flown down the tree. Out into the orchard he dashed, to try to break the mirror's fall, but whether he arrived in time I could not see, it was so dark. My eyes remained on Timothy, who'd no sooner let the mirror go than plucked a candle from its cup and then himself jumped headlong out into the blackness, down toward the spot where he knew Odin and the mirror would meet. Down plunged his tiny flame into the night, and where he landed, I could see only the tip of his candle, thrashing round and back like a furious lightning bug caught in a jar. Then for an instant it seemed to disappear. All was black and silent. I heard a gasp, and suddenly a great conflagration burst out, the shape of a man consumed by flame. It staggered into the orchard, arms and legs ablaze, then fell to the ground and was gone. All was dark again but for a gray cloud of smoke which rose into the sky, and just beneath it a fragile ashen bracelet floating up and up, hovering there above the trees, and then falling down like a feather.

The one who'd survived was still in the brush, I could hear him gasping for air. Quickly I stood up from my bench and stepped into the light shed by the tree.

"Hello," I called out. "Hello, do you need any help?" I listened, but there was only the wind in the orchard. I took a step toward the brush, and then at the light's edge, an arm appeared, all black and charred. I went to help. I lifted him up, and I could see now, it was Timothy—but how light he was, he might have blown from my arms. I carried him beneath the tree and laid him on the levelest surface I could find. His left arm was all charred. He'd lost his right leg entirely, and he was having difficulty breathing. "Is there anything I can do?" I asked.

He looked down at his injuries and shook his head, then turned away slightly. He extended his blackened arm and clenched his fist. A terrible low gasp issued from his paper mouth, and the entire limb collapsed on the moss in ashes.

I heard him whisper, "The mirror, please."

It was still out in the orchard. I could see the flame of his candle flickering on the ground, and found the mirror just to the side— a very plain mirror, with a round face and a handle made of wood. I brought it back beneath the tree.

"Is it broken?" murmured Timothy.

"No," I said. "It seems to be perfectly intact."

He nodded, then looked out into the black orchard as if others might be out there waiting for him. "A favor?" he asked.

"Yes?"

"Break it."

For a moment I hesitated; it seemed like a strange desire after so fierce a battle.

"Please," he whispered.

I took the mirror over to the creek and dropped a heavy stone three times on the glass before it shattered. Then I brought the mirror back to Timothy. He looked at the fractured reflection of his face and his whole body seemed to ease.

"Now." He looked up into the boughs of the tree, and his voice was just the breeze, guided through his body and out his mouth. "I need you to cut away my cinders." He reached down to touch where his hip was burned open. The edges were all puckered, flaked and ashen.

I took my kerchief and wrapped it around my fingers to pick a shard from the mirror frame, then with its sharp edge I sliced all the black and useless paper from Timothy's body.

When I had finished, he looked down at his open hip and shoulder and nodded his thanks. Then he extended his good arm out to the side, opened his hand, and stared at it a moment. The main seam of his palm flipped open, the fingers unfolded, and the whole of his hand lay creased and open like foil.

He looked up at me, and his voice as he spoke was weaker yet. He had to wait for the breeze. "I am going to unfold now," he said, "and try to find another form." He paused again, then as the limbs creaked above us, he instructed me in a whisper: "When I am opened, place the shards upon me and stay the night. If I've not returned by morning, take the last burning candle from the tree and set the page afire." He laid his head back gently on the moss.

"Very well," I said, and I waited. The whole night and every candle in the candletree waited, and then it began. Like the petals of a flower opening, the seams came undone at his elbow and at his shoulder. I looked down at his good leg and the same became of his paper foot. His ankle and calf opened, his knee unfolded. All the intricate pleats which had provided his agility, the origami knight spread out by will, until the only features of his body that remained were his torso and his head. One last time he looked up to see the glowing tree above him, lest he not return, then laid his head back down, and with only the sound of paper scuffing against itself—no cry or whimper—his chest opened out, his neck and then his face unwrapped, and he was gone.

I looked down at the paper now—an envelope torn brutally open, with nothing inside. As he'd asked, I placed the shards of the mirror on top, then sat and waited, unaware of how long it should take for his life to leave or to return. All around me, the candle drips began to fall on their own, down along their stalks and onto the castles below.

I did what I could to pass the time. I studied my map; I prayed (without petition); I swept the ashes of Timothy's arm and sprinkled them in the creek, but still the paper did not move. I returned to my map, and prayed some more (this time with petition), but found no answer. The page lay flat beneath the weeping tree.

I am afraid that my exhaustion then got the better of me. I fell asleep, I don't know for how long, but it was nearly dawn when I awoke. I could see the daylight was ready to begin its slow ascent from the horizon but the paper was just as I'd left it. Some of the counters had already begun to stir, as if waking from a slumber. All the candles were desperately low in their cups, and some were flickering out already, streaming up thin trails of smoke.

I looked for the tallest. I stood up to inspect the lowest branches, and from the corner of my eye I saw the paper's edge move ever so slightly. The wind, I thought. I could hear it stirring the orchard. But then one of the corners rose higher, and all at once the paper came to life. Its two sharp corners reached out over the shards of glass to meet, and then, as if some invisible hand were there to flatten it, a crease appeared along the edge. The page opened and closed again, rose up like a diamond, then narrowed its lower tips, which turned up inside themselves. One of these reversed again, as the two top corners both pulled down, and I could see that they were wings, and that by this very simple dance, this half-consumed white sheet of paper, which the night before had rendered such an exquisite paladin, had transformed before my eyes into an origami crane.

He awoke with a gentle flap of his wings, and lifted forward sluggishly. He bent his head to see the form he'd taken, then beat his wings a second time, but the dripcastles were in his way. I thought he'd need a clearing, so I went and picked him up.

By now an orange glow was creeping up the sky. Every candle in the tree had gone out. The counters had all awakened and were rolling off into the orchard, all but my red friend who was standing out by the rows, waiting. I brought him the the crane in my arms, and we turned and followed the others through the trees. They kept circling around behind us, begging us to hurry, and the crane was struggling in my arms. He beat his wings in protest, and I could hear the shards of glass slide inside his belly, but I held fast until we came to the orchard's edge.

There was bluff beside the sea, covered in a thick blanket of white flowers. The counters raced out ahead, all bumping up and down and leaving thin trails behind, but my red friend remained with me. Together we walked the crane out into the middle of the meadow and as we felt the winds sweep around us, I let Timothy free from my arms.

He dropped down at first. His belly whisked the tops of the flowers, but then a breeze swept underneath him, and with another strum he rose higher. Higher and higher, he beat his paper wings. He turned a wide circle above us, and, as he flew out beyond the cliff, was met by stronger winds which threw him straight upward, so high and far I knew he wouldn't be returning to us. He soared out above the ocean, and from the bluff I stood and watched him grow smaller and smaller, until he disappeared entirely inside the morning blue sky. Where he shall land, where he shall fly his precious shards, I suppose I'll never know.

I miss you all. I think of you. Now go home and sleep, and say a prayer that Timothy lands among friends.

Good night,
Gus

•

Three days after the reading of the doctor's letter, a paper crane with a slightly burned tail and little shards of glass in its belly was found by Mr. Thomas E. Thomas. It had apparently landed on his lap while he was enjoying an afternoon nap on one of the sunny benches by the Holt Street fence.

Of Castles

José Ferrer surveys a game in the film Anything Can Happen, *1952.*

and Kings

Chess Across the Board

Medieval version of a scene in Homer's Odyssey: *Achilles plays chess during the siege of Troy. (Miniature painting, late 14th century.)*

Set designed by Man Ray, 1926.

James Mason plays chess with
Shelley Winters in Lolita, 1962.

Boxwood set designed by Max Ernst, 1944. The queens are 5 inches tall and the kings 4 1/2.

Below: Gallery proprietor Julien Levy (right) plays against gallery assistant Ruth Steinrich on the Max Ernst set, January 1945.

Marcel Duchamp and his wife, Teeny, play against John Cage at the "Reunion" Concert in Toronto, 1968.

Actress Barbara Read plays with the "Lipstick" set, Hollywood, 1937.

James Dean plays solitaire on a pocket set in his dressing room on the set of Rebel Without a Cause, *1955.*

*Leather and celluloid pocket set designed by
Marcel Duchamp, 1943.*

...Automaton Chess-Playing Machine, invented by ...gang von Kempelen in 1769. A clever fraud— ...ally operated by a man concealed in the cabinet. ...graving, 1847.)

Boris Karloff challenges Bela Lugosi on the set of The Black Cat, *Hollywood, 1934.*

An outdoor game with lacquered foam rubber pieces in Moers recreation park,
West Germany, 1978.

Christian Lebanese Forces militiamen, wearing masks of French president François Mitterrand and Iranian leader Ayatollah Khomeini, play chess at Beirut's green-line battlefront, 1987.

Right: 20th-century Russian set depicting Capitalists vs. Communists.

Set designed by London taxi driver John Robertson in 1975, depicting important figures in World War II history. Included are Eva Braun, Bernard Montgomery, Winston Churchill, Erwin Rommel, Queen Elizabeth, Adolf Hitler, Hermann Goering, and King George VI.

U.S. Marine Corps members in Saudi Arabia during the Gulf War play chess with a set constructed from water bottles and soda cans, 1990.

Clockwise from top left:

Chess grand masters O'Kelly de Galway and Georg Kieninger "move" human pieces through loudspeaker commands, Eupen, Belgium, 1960.

20th-century Nigerian set with goatskin board.

Boatbuilder and inventor Ken Mobert plays on the three-way "Interface" chess board he designed, 1972.

American Indian Movement members play with a set made with .357 magnum, .45 automatic, 30.06, and .38 special shells, Wounded Knee, South Dakota, 1973.

A floating chess board at the Szabadsag open-air swimming pool in Budapest, 1962.

German "Fish Life" set in Meissen porcelain designed by Max Esser, 1925.

A floating chess board carries actresses Anne Rondags and Françoise Thuries, Port Grimaud, France, 1972.

Arctic Hegira

On the first run through
there's no hint, none
of the crimp
so free a disturbance
of air might bear. But
by the fifth repeat
silences freeze
the loop shut, there
is nervous experimentation
with starting, so, slow,
or moving on, too fast, as if
one could hex change
out of the scheme.
In time, a beat, one gives in.
If it really has to be done
then it might as well be done
well; what needs to be done
may be accomplished
with style, even verve. To crimp is to gash
the flesh of a fish, to make it crisp
when cooked. To be crimped
is to feel those gashes, to think oneself
into the knife, the skin, the pattern so
random, so imposed.
In time, one's own, one
breaks,
free. What
was soundly bound

shatters, all jag now,
shrapnel, in hap-
hazard, dissonant flight
to far corners of meaning, and
because, simply
because
that can't last, a
coming together, in the sound
one's breath makes in the arctic,
as ice crystals form,
and fall, in
tinkling
accord.

From *Berlin Childhood in Nineteen Hundred*

The Merry-Go-Round

The board spins, with its subservient animals just above the ground, at the height at which you fly best in dreams. Music begins, and the child jolts away from his mother. At first he is scared to be leaving her. But then he realizes how loyal he is. From his throne, he reigns over a world that belongs to him. Around the rotary, trees and natives form a guard of honor. Then, in the Orient, his mother surfaces again. Next, a treetop rises from the jungle—one the child saw millenniums ago just as he sees it now, on the merry-go-round. His animal is fond of him: Like a mute Arion, he rides a mute fish or, like the immaculate Europa, he is abducted by a wooden bull-Zeus. The eternal return of all things has long since become a childhood wisdom, and life is an ancient intoxication of dominance with its royal treasure, the booming orchestrion, at its center. As its playing slows, the room begins to stutter and the trees have second thoughts. The merry-go-round becomes precarious ground. His mother reappears, the strongly rooted pole around which the landing child winds the rope of his gaze.

Butterfly Hunting

Every summer before I began attending school, and aside from occasional summer trips, we moved to some house in the surrounding countryside. These houses were evoked, for a long time, by the spacious box on the wall of my boyhood room—a box that held the rudiments of a butterfly collection, the oldest exemplars of which had been netted in the garden on Brauhausberg, "Mount Brewery." Cabbage butterflies with sloughed-off edges, brimstones with overly shiny wings, conjured up the passionate hunts that so often lured me away from the manicured garden paths to a wilderness where I was powerless against the conspiracy of wind and scents, leaves and sun, that worked to control the flight of the butterflies.

They fluttered toward a blossom, they hovered above it. With a raised net, I waited only until the spell the blossom seemed to cast on the pair of wings had done its work; then, the delicate body would slip out with gentle side thrusts, and shade another blossom just as motionlessly and, without touching it, leave it just as suddenly. If such a tortoiseshell or privet hawkmoth that I might have comfortably overtaken made a fool of me by wavering, hesitating, and lingering, then I longed to dissolve in light and air, simply so I could sneak up on my prey and overpower it. And my wish came true. Every swing or sway of the wings I was crazy about, wafting toward me, gave me the shivers. The ancient hunting laws took effect between us: the closer I nestled with all my fibers against the animal

and the more butterfly-like my mind became, the more the butter-fly, in all it did, took on the color of human resolution, and ulti-mately I felt that catching it would be the only way to regain my human existence. But once I had netted it, I had to go back along an arduous road from the place of my hunting success to the camp where ether, cotton, tweezers, and needles with colored heads emerged from the specimen box. And imagine the condition of the hunting ground I had left behind! Crushed grass, trampled flowers, the hunter himself had thrown his body after his net; and through all that destruction, barbarity, and violence, the terrified butterfly stayed quivering, gracefully, in a fold of the net. It was along this arduous road that the spirit of the doomed creature passed into the hunter. And he managed to glean a few rules of the foreign tongue in which this butterfly and the blossoms it confronted had commu-nicated. He had grown all the less bloodthirsty, all the more confident.

The air in which that butterfly hovered is now thoroughly im-bued with a word that has not reached my ears or crossed my lips in decades. It has preserved the inscrutability of childhood names that grownups do not understand. That word has been transfigured by a long hush. The air that is filled with butterflies quivers with the word *Brauhausberg*. We had our summer house on "Mount Brewery" near Potsdam. But the name has lost all gravity, it has nothing left of a brewery and is at most a mountain veiled in blue, a mountain that loomed up each summer to house me and my parents. And that is why the Potsdam of my childhood lies in deep blue air, as if its mourning cloaks and red admirals, its peacocks and orange tips, had been scattered over one of those shimmering Limoges porcelains on which the merlons and ramparts of Jerusalem loom brightly against a dark-blue background.

Hiding Places

I already knew all the hiding places in our home and returned to them the way you return to a house where you are certain to find everything as it was before. My heart pounded. I held my breath. Here, I was enclosed in the material world. It was tremendously clear to me, grew close to me wordlessly. That is how a man who is hanged first realizes what rope and wood are. The child standing behind the portière becomes something wafting and white, a ghost. The dining-room table under which he crouches transforms him into the

wooden idol in a temple, its carved legs becoming the temple's four columns. And behind a door, he himself is a door, wears the door like a heavy mask and, as shaman, will cast a spell on all who enter unknowingly. On no account must he be found. If he makes faces, he is told that the clock only needs to strike and his grimace will remain. I found the truth of that warning in my hiding places. Anyone who discovered me could petrify me forever as an idol under the table, weave me as a ghost into the curtain, spellbind me lifelong into the heavy door. So when the seeker grabbed me, I let out a loud shriek, expelling the demon who had transformed me—indeed, I did not even wait for the exact moment, I anticipated it with a shriek of self-liberation. I never tired of fighting the demon. Our home became an arsenal of masks. But once a year, presents lay in mysterious places, in the hollow eye sockets of the masks, in their rigid mouths. The magical experience became a science. I, as its engineer, broke the spell of my parents' dark home and hunted for Easter eggs.

Translated from the German by Joachim Neugroschel

nostalgia

could see the wedding guests step out of the house if i craned my neck, he said, if i stood on tiptoe and looked out the high transoms, down where they were yelling as if everybody were deaf, it drifted up to me, right in the outworks, coat, cape, loden, march-chill.

if i braced myself and on tiptoe, he said, neck craned, i could see them all, they had all come out of the house, inside they had been sitting, capetown brown, between crocheted antimacassars, on rattan rockers, he said, always.

if i craned my neck i could see them push out of the house to get some air, could hear them yell, and the aunts from capetown with their kinky hair.

if i strained i could see them all, yelling and wanting to get out of the house, holding flowers, all of them, to get some air, he said, at that time i had already stopped sneering at things, he said.

with craned neck i could survey the yelling crowd pushing out of the house to get some air, a dream of course, he said, and the wintery twitter of birds high above me, giant green aviary.

if i stood on tiptoe i could see them all, he said, american magazines, the african aunt had told me, give reading time in number of subway stations, a dream of course, he said, march-chill.

balancing on tiptoe i saw them push out of the house, a delirium perhaps, he said, a new penetration of reality, he said, an utmost determination, he said, a suicidal rage, he said.

craned my neck, saw them all push outside for a bit of air, he said, saw them speak orientish, verbhose, nimble languages, he said, a dream of course, all tables occupied, they yelled, shall we wait here, they yelled, shall we sit down over there, they yelled.

stretched and saw them almost make a move to turn this way or that in order to sit down, he said, a dream of course, march-chill, he said, to the rhine! they yelled, all the while crowding in front of the house where the air was steaming, and i heard them yell up to my observation post, look, they yelled, how the dome is being blown off the ramp, look, gusts of rough air, shadowy *beuel*, a dream of course, may-stockinged thin the bride, right in the outworks, suddenly shadows.

if i braced myself, craned my neck, i could observe everything precisely, suddenly shadows, he said, and how the bride and the bridegroom, and how they all yelled louder again, the group photo! they yelled at one another, get on with the group photo!

craned my neck, finally the group photo, he said, and again the group photo, group photo of the capetown-brown aunts, the other brown aunts, the old masters always arranged it, he said, so that the heads formed a wavy line, a dream of course, he said.

straining upwards i could follow everything precisely, the group photo, the old masters, they composed this way, he said, a dream of course, heads in a wavy line, a scatter of events.

if i craned my neck i saw them slowly begin to turn away, he said, a dream of course, the scatter of events, the scatter of events is amazing when seen from above, he said, the scatter of events, and how every new day we wash, dress, have washed, have dressed, this torture till we've finished washing, dressing, and how we can't bear being talked to in the morning, he said, could this not go so far, he said, that we'd no longer want to set foot into the morning, he said, at least from my post of observation, he said.

on tiptoe, the clan as if transformed into images, he said, if i brace myself, a dream of course, the clan now finally drying up, he said, the group dispersing more and more, flocking toward the rhine, at least all out of the house, he said, a dream of course, when i stood at the cash register and did not look at the bills handed to me, but instead tried to interpret the smile of the woman at the next cash register, a dream of course, rhineward, he said, at least all out of the house now.

craned my neck, but transformations are necessary, he said, transformed into images, how they scattered along the bank, he said, and when the clan had finally dried up, he said, a cork out of a giant bottle, he said, i called to the oldest relative, though she could not hear me all the way down there, miss misa, i called, miss misa—with this branch of the family we've always been formal—do you remember, miss misa, i called again, he said, do you remember. yes, she said, a dream of course, for she could not possibly hear me from up here, he said. yes, she said softly, in the women's auxiliary together with your mother, forty-two to forty-five.

again surveyed the whole clan, straining, he said, saw them draw closer and closer to the banks of the rhine, the rhine black with crows fluttering above, and on a billboard nearby a poster kept coming off even though one of the group kept striking it with his fist to fix it, again and again, he said, air *schlieren.*

craning upwards, i could see they now had scattered completely, a second's compulsion, heading in various directions and definitely making the group photo impossible, roses from picardy, a dream of course, and now it was coming down with a splash, the whole width of the embankment. above me they started screaming again, winter birds, heads tossed back, a dream of course, black crows, he said, the course of events, he said, miss misa, i said, the course of events, it's a matter of the course of events.

bracing myself, he said, i can hear and see their voices like shadows in the distance, he said, a dream of course, and now, now i see them all together again, hurrying toward the anchorage, transformed back into solid form, into a single figure, the anchorage swaying and veiled, thistles in their hair, a dream of course, he said, thistles in their hair.

Translated from the German by Rosmarie Waldrop

CHRIS BURDEN

America's Darker Moments

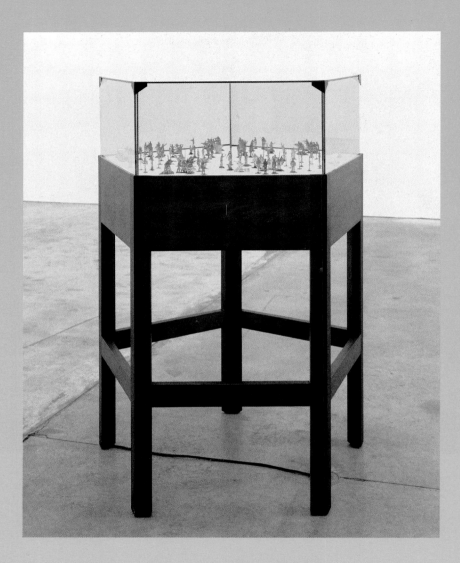

America's Darker Moments, 1994
Figures: cast tin with paint. Vitrine: wood, plexiglas, glass, fluorescent lights.
56 ½ x 36 ½ x 36 ½ inches.
Following pages: details from above.

The Killing of Kent State Students by National Guardsmen

The My Lai Massacre, Vietnam

The Assassination of John F. Kennedy

The Murder of Emmett Till

The Bombing of Hiroshima

America's Darker Moments

In *America's Darker Moments* (1994), an installation at the Gagosian Gallery in New York, Chris Burden recreates Kent State, My Lai, the assassination of John F. Kennedy, the murder of Emmett Till, and the bombing of Hiroshima, in a series of miniature pewter dioramas posed in a five-sided vitrine. Although the work's pentagonal cabinet refers directly to the military, Burden deals also with political, religious, and community situations. Divided by mirrored partitions and lit from below, Burden's figures are reminiscent of playthings, toy soldiers or pieces on a game board, that act out some of the most chilling or tragic moments of recent American history.

Menace

Lonely gondolas blacken canals
like black shoes floating away
from a funeral. Big-nosed gargoyles
shade their own lips.

Crooked as a fiddler's elbow—
and a pederast priest—
is the way to a Latin mass.
The fruit has fallen, the leaf is stiff.

Alleluiah, alleluiah.

Noted

When Adam the Billionth
called the sky's name
he was like someone who believed
his voice made him a magician.

Psychoanalysis had no cure—
and neither did America—for his error.
Nothing! he shouted
and the print this word left in the air

was as gray as moonstuff
and the world was dimmer for it.
We shall all fall into Tophet
like ice off of fruit

before anyone answers to that name.

Billy and Girl: Games

Soon all the kids in England will be pushing up daisies. That's what Girl says every night before I go to sleep. Girl is my sister and I'm scared of her. She's got ice in her veins and seams on her stockings and tonight she reads me my rights.

"Billy," she says in that voice like turpentine, "you have the right to drown. You have the right to shoot someone with your gun and you have the right to a telephone call. Which one is it to be?" Yesterday she bought me a present. A pair of stacked red sneakers wrapped in folds of white tissue paper. She likes me to look like a baby gangster and I don't mind, but now I have to pay for them. My sister pretends to be retarded sometimes so she doesn't have to speak or react like other people do. Then just when you think she is in Neverland, she suddenly springs on you with her white-trash fists.

Girl was in love once. She was nice to me then and bought me a badminton set for us to play in the park. She was just bowled over by all that kissing she did in restaurants, wine stains on the table-cloth, ashtrays overflowing with her gold-band butts. It made her high enough to sing and jump and swipe the shuttlecock back to me with the toy racket. Her sweetheart was called Prince and they were so in love they drove around in a car that had rotting lamb chops in the trunk, bought for supper but forgotten, and though the car smelt like a steaming abattoir to everyone else, Girl and

Prince couldn't smell it—that's how somewhere else they were. He bought me a water pistol and I shot myself in the ear, up the nostrils, in my heart, and on the inside of my thigh, each death more spectacular than the last, watched by the neighborhood cats with their spacey eyes.

"Which one are you going to choose, Billy?" Girl's black eyes, always vacant, conveniently give the impression she is brain damaged.

I am in the womb of my mother who will later disappear without a trace. "Don't cry," Girl chides me, twisting her thin lips.

I am in the womb of my mother. I hear car alarms go off and sometimes hear my father. He says, "Hello, babykins. This is your daddy speaking. We are looking forward to meeting you, over and out." I hear cats purring and Girl shouting, "You're late, brother. Come on out!" I don't want to be born. I'm never coming out. Dad tries again: "Hello, babykins, it's your daddy here. Time to face the world like a man—looking forward to meeting you, son. Over and out."

Girl strokes my head, babying me like she sometimes does. I'd like to eat something with onions in it. Pizza or soup. Like Mom used to make before she disappeared. The night before she had me, she swam in shorty pajamas and ate cinnamon buns. Life could have been amazing. We could have gone together to the video shop and bought ice cream, jelly beans, and micro popping corn. We could have sat at home and watched a film, sprawled on the floor, stuffing ourselves.

Girl says, "No, boy, that is someone else's memory. We never went to a video shop."

When Robocop says, "Stay out of trouble," I listen to him, but the trouble is in my head. It's in my chest and the back of my neck. Dad pulled into a gas station. He put the pump into his mouth and got £5 worth. Then he took out his cigarettes and lit up. It was the biggest barbecue South London had ever seen. My father had never smoked before. This was his first and last cigarette and his suicide was the most splendid thing he did in his life. Girl and I have talked about it over and over. We decided he must have bought the pack from the newsstand near the Odeon. Coins cold in his hand. Black secret in his heart. Streatham's lone cowboy without horse or bourbon, just an imagination expressed for the first time. All the people coming out of the Esso shop clutching sausage rolls and cans of Fanta fell about screaming. A reporter from a newspaper offered Mom the chance to "open her heart to the world." Afterward she bought Girl a Cindy doll with long blond hair, a blue bikini, a little pearl necklace, and a plastic Ferrari with silver wheels. We set fire to Cindy one night and watched her melt before our eyes. Then I went off to watch Looney Tunes outside the TV shop in the mall.

After I was born Mom took special pain killers because they cut her up at the hospital to pull me out. Cross your heels like a cat, the midwife said, and yanked out the placenta with both hands. I lay on Mom's breast and they stitched her up while Dad cried in the corridor, eventually putting his head round the door and whispering, "All right, love?" When Mom took me home she examined my fingernails first. "Look, Girl," she said, "they've grown right to the edge and over." So I would scratch my face with sharp nails. Make little fists and raise them to my cheeks and scratch because it upset Mom and made her kiss me more. She'd sit in a blue bucket under the shower, the smell of lavender she had added to the water filling the steamy corridor where Girl and I sat waiting for her. "The lavender fields of Provence, Billy, that's what you can smell," she shouted through the steam, and Girl and I watched the rain splash against the windows, shivering in our secondhand T-shirts.

After she had bathed her birth wounds she limped downstairs to make Girl breakfast: banana fritters. Girl wanted banana everything. Banana milkshakes, banana blancmange, banana curry. Mom was a bit nervous of Girl and catered to her compulsions for fear she would weep those catastrophic tears of hers and never stop. When Girl cries, the world slows down. It's like her thin white body is going to snap in two because her grief is so total and infinite. In the days we used to go for rides in the country, if she didn't see a horse she'd scream and shout as if somehow this was a bad omen and the sky was going to fall on her head. Dad would get desperate and point to a cow grazing in a field. "There's a horsie, Girl, see?" The lie seemed to comfort her, as if just naming the beast completed the magic circle in her ash-white head, and she would calm down and fall asleep.

Girl has always invented games for me and her to play together. Her favorite used to be the bolt game. When she found a jar full of two-inch wrought iron bolts in the cupboard under the stairs where all the nails and screws were kept, she showed them to me as if she had found gold in a cave. All day she brooded on what to do with them, hiding behind her fringe of white hair when anyone dared speak to her.

"It's a pain game, Billy," she whispered when Mom went out of the room and the next thing I knew she had dragged me outside and was drawing a chalk line on the pavement which I had to stand behind. Then she measured twenty footsteps away from my line and drew another line which she stood behind. I had to keep completely still while she aimed the little bolts at my head. When they missed and got me on my shins or on my fingertips I was not allowed to cry. It was a pain game after all, and success was measured by how stoic the person being hit could be. The day Girl broke the skin on my forehead and blood dripped down my face and onto my T-shirt, she screamed, "Don't blink, Billy," and then hugged me for being so hard. "You're a hero," she said in her acid-drop voice, and licked the warm blood with her tongue while I pretended to meow like a kitten.

A few weeks after Dad set fire to himself at the gas station, Mom took me on a coach trip somewhere near Newcastle station to meet my grandfather. That's my father's father. She packed tuna sandwiches and a flask of tea and sat me on her knee in the coach so she wouldn't have to pay for another ticket. I swear I could smell rubber on the tarmac of the motorway and the milk in Mom's breast, and when we arrived we heard a fat man in a pub sing *England! Awake! Awake! Awake!* I lay on her lap under the little tartan blanket and scratched my eyelids all the time, remembering my dad whispering, "Hell-oo, babykins, it's your father here, over and out," scratch scratch, and Mom catching my fingers tight in her hands. Granddad talked in whispers to Mom, sometimes leaning over me with his watery eyes and beery breath, checking me out and looking away again, and I swear by the time he gave Mom three green tomatoes grown on his plot of land instead of the money I knew she wanted, I thought, "Jeez, I really need a cigarette."

"You are my balaclava angel," Girl whispers to me as I hold up the mirror for her while she trims her bangs. No, I'm not. I'm a broken-hearted bastard. I want to be the bloke on the Häagen-Dazs ads, with good-looking girls in their underwear pouring ice cream all over my big beautiful body. Instead I'm poor, white, and stupid. I take my knife into cinemas and stab the velvet seats in the dark. That is my silent broadcast to the British nation. At night I hide in small gardens outside here and count the TV aerials. I click the heels of my new red sneakers three times, take a deep breath, hold my nose, and wait for the wind to take me somewhere better than this.

A Deep-Sea Explorer
of the Mind

*Birger Sellin was born on February 1, 1973 in West Berlin. His early
development was normal. He was an outgoing, happy child who began to
talk at an early age. In October 1974, his parents sent him to his first half-
day of nursery school. When they came to pick him up, he began screaming and could not be calmed down. Soon afterward, he developed a
middle-ear inflammation and was ill for three months. By the time he
recovered, he had changed drastically. He screamed whenever he had to
leave the house and panicked at the sight of other children. His command
of language began to deteriorate and his vocabulary shrank steadily. He
soon stopped talking entirely. He no longer responded to his parents and
he avoided all eye contact. After six months of therapy at the Wiesengrund
Psychiatric Hospital, he had made no improvement. A case report diag-
nosed him as "probably suffering from postencephalitic retardation," or
mental retardation brought on by an inflammation of the brain cells.*

*When Birger was brought home from the hospital, he made no attempt
to communicate or react; he sat in the living room, usually underneath
the dining table, constantly rocking his upper body. He spent most of his
time absorbed in the rigid, repetitive action of leafing through books he
pulled down from his parents' shelves. At four and a half, he was diag-
nosed at the Free University of Berlin as "autistic." In 1977, the German
Society for Autistic Children was established in West Berlin and Birger*

attended its Early Development program, where he learned to eat, wash, dress, brush his teeth, and go to the toilet by himself. He gradually became more independent, but still did not speak. He abandoned books for marbles and glass beads, which he would run through his hands for hours at a time. Although he had hundreds of marbles, he noticed instantly if one was missing: he would become restless and search frantically for it. The marbles also provided the occasion for the only sentence Birger has so far uttered. When his father, playing with him, took one of the marbles, Birger demanded in a clear, strong voice, "Give me that ball back!" He never spoke again.

At the onset of puberty, Birger became harder to cope with. He lived in an increasingly hectic state. He had screaming fits, he bit and hit himself until he drew blood. He ran frantically around the house, wet his bed, and ate any food he could find. At the same time, he remained mute, seemingly uninterested and without understanding of what was going on around him. By the time he was eighteen, he was regarded as incurably insane.

In 1990, his parents heard of the therapy known as facilitated communication: in an effort to overcome the psychological or communication block common in autistics, someone the patient trusts sits at a typewriter or computer keyboard with the patient and supports his lower arm. This external aid gives him the confidence and strength to press the keys with his index finger and express himself in writing. As time goes on, mechanical support can be either withdrawn entirely or reduced to a hand laid on the writer's shoulder.

In the beginning, Birger typed only isolated words. His parents began by getting him to identify photographs and pictures, members of his family, animals, household items. On September 8, 1990, thirteen days after he began writing, he wrote to his mother, "i love you." One can hardly begin to imagine Annemarie Sellin's feelings when she read those words after sixteen years of silence. Almost every evening since then, Birger has written at the computer in his parents' study, usually with his mother supporting him. The selection here ends in 1992. Birger is still writing.

—Michael Klonovsky

abcdefghijklmnopqrstuvwxyz
birger papa jonasmama*

8.27.1990

carr grandpa and grandma jonas tookit packet
pockets wettblgghnukoa
father mother brotther mmölln
peepl
stopnow owllglass

8.30.1990

duuck duck
packet nest eggs
mask basket caaamel camel
hedgehog cucumber grass
i would like tosstop to sstop

9.7.1990

packet telephone lamp arm pen
car ball apple cow foot bed traffic light
scissors locomotive ladder spooon
i dont i want tto stop
i love youyes

9.8.1990

please to bedd

9.25.1990

im going toslee sleep
going to sleep

9.26.1990

can i eat whats
on all the plates

9.29.1990

---

* Jonas, Birger's younger brother.

imm a hobljl
im a gorri
gorribte
rrrrinn
horink
horrible person

10.16.1990

i wannt to go home
can hagg
simpply habv good time
you shl should
like firdud more since everyone ss
says youre so kind
itss the sas sadhc
saysso letssa
sd begin t GETTING BETTER Fs sosf
wo so t ta take care
b but biirger can
t get anywhere without love
all a ft
ut yt uts just vr very
very very dear aw aaberb barsr af
area say
asay that you loveme
ss say ay that you all jonas too and dannkward* adw aswell
all i liiike specially anne adc
whenyou sclded
scold bsys bahs soals

10.22.1990

today was letsay kindof
a and not act the way
i llike it because im different from other people
but id rather not be that way
other people say im handicapped

11.4.1990

---

* Dankward, Birger's father.

cc can i call people crazt crazy so
i dont have to liike
nobody liket crrraxy people

11.9.1990

you must help me to talk
you mh must gol hold my arm
ththe question is will we be able to talk clearly enough
only when we are really
a all died dead get our shpe of being
the way we want it
thats why i often wish i was dead
because im alone in my loneliness

11.24.1990

you mustnt scold but today
you were very pattient i dont fit into the widde world atall
because im afraid im
just afraid of
ordinary things that seem as hala harmless
as buildings
well they seem threatening to me im always scared
but today it was specially bad becc
be cause you shouted at me like that today i couldnt
do up my coat
it bothered me so much bb
its not really so bad
then it gets bad when im scared i think thats crazy but
once i couldnt find my bead
zannd 1 but nothing bad happened
wh which is why im stupid when im scared its ve ry
stupid when
okay so you cnn laugh when
i scream out loud but yyou did tht that long before i
could talk

11.25.1990

im no notthing nothing atall

12.9.1990

solomon was a wise king i know it all only i cant say it in fact its only in writing i can say things at speed i mean lets say fast i can say things that scare people but i dont do that ive often been scared because people didnt know i understand everything so they just said everything i wasnt supposed to be hearing i only liked being at those parties in the world at the time but otherwise i thought up all kinds of things so i could get out of that way of being the silliest idea was when i thought it could all be switched off now i dont need those methods any more because now i can write so thats that i never said so much before as i did today but now its a pity its over

12.13.1990

astronomy is about the stars but i dont believe in the stars because it isnt likely that constellations could give advice lets say it can be proved that the earth is only lets say a structure in space

12.14.1990

achim* was lets say asocial yes that word is taken out say what you like it still makes no sense what kind of sense would it make the fact is achim was very social asocial if you are explaining things about adaptation we all have to keep adapting to a social system but almost everything we actually do is a kind of adaptation darwin was the first person to work on that subject which as you might expect he lets say deduced from his ideas that social species are inherited its a fact but the species say something about the social nature of races seeds are crossed

12.17.1990

i want something which i just cant learn from any creature in this world im bursting with restlessness and impatience i would so much like to find my way out of my isolated life out of decadent

---

* A case helper at the Center with whom Birger has a particularly close relationship.

ways of behaving which i use like armor i feel only frustration day in day out without hope in this life of ever being lifted out or wiped out of this hopeless isolation or having it wiped out i cant make a just a little socalled tiny problem out of the very weighty lets say serious facts of isolation the fact is it is technically impossible its almost sure not to succeed

12.25.1990

lisbon madrid dar es salaam panamaribo*
yes i am glad but i can see all that about school is ridiculous because i am a restless spirit i show no obvious understanding if a miracle happened lets say this restless spirit became calmer

---

*Birger told his parents (on the keyboard) that he knew all the capital cities of the world.

articulated better so that everyone could understand what he was
saying the way speaking people easily understand each other then
all the same its a fact it would be too difficult for me but i havent
entirely given up that hope

12.29.1990

i dont want to do sums because i am too big i am big and
clever and handicapped
i am a sad case
they tied me down in the hospital at night*
didnt you like coming to see me every day then
anyway i dont want to be handicapped

1.7.1991

amsterdam oslo warshawa warsaw
today i am going to tell a story once upon a time in a lonely little
town there lived a wonderful young woman she was very sad
because she was so alone she was a poor widow and had nobody
in the world but along came another man and married her on
the spot and they lived a loving poor life so that they didnt mind
anything in the world as they were sitting there along came a
darkness from the atmosphere and the air turned dreadfully
sticky so that no one dared to breathe any more its a fact they all
died but i will go on with this story tomorrow because it is much
too long.

1.13.1991

i will tell some more of that story
when the darkness scared people they saw nothing after that
everything was wrapped in darkness but there were more and
more people wandering around in the streets if an accident happened no one could help anyone else but if a like massive disas-
ter i mean a gigantic misfortune happened then they got in a

---

* Birger is referring to his stay in the Wiesengrund children's hospital.

panic many of them were really dead there wasnt any house where nothing happened they were all gone underground for socalled security reasons unfortunately water came bubbling up from the depths and a lot of people were drowned and there were fabulous apparitions over the earth too which scared the rest of them savage pterodactyls attacked the globe its a fact that very large species from primeval times appeared just like it said in the bible

1.15.1991

no one talks worse nonsense thats to say it is less foolish than jaksson* who is a lets say pop singer he is so exciting i saw him on television he was singing a song about keasatsad yes that means the world is made for you and not for soldiers we mustnt allow everything on earth to be bombed when i heard that strong song sung fast in haste i had an ejaculation for the first time ive been lets say a fan of jakssons ever since then

1.19.1991

chemistry is exciting but id rather do biology this semester† but dont worry i think i will soon be enjoying a lot of other subjects

2.16.1991

i dont want to be inside me anymore
i have eyes and i can see so i have been terribly scared and so i didnt want to say any more
about that
i was afraid of the end of the road and the end of humanity

3.7.1991

i dont fit into this crazy cowardly horrible society it is so weird this selection of strong ace performers

3.9.1991

---

* The singer Michael Jackson.

† Birger's parents are asking him questions on various academic subjects to find out what he has read. As it turns out, he has a photographic memory and has been reading the books they assumed he was simply "leafing through."

do you really know how deep-rooted anxiety can be in an
individual
the way it eats away at an individual
the way it works personally on a single person at the
collapse of the first agonizing words
it is like total perception
the meadows will be green the sun will certainly be
shining brightly if the anxiety goes away
for just a minute
it is kind of an incredible way to improve values a simple
momentary glance into eternity
a totally monstrous light in total darkness

6.24.1991

the way one of your sons upset you today will certainly
never ever happen again
if you are going to react like that another time without
good reason then a state of agitation
is really important and it is none of my doing so you will
see there is no point getting
so obviously upset
i thought our jonas was lost you see*

6.30.1991

its a fact i wanted to find my own way home†
first i went by subway to the crooked lanke
and various subways i knew the avus was further on
its so hard to find your way
it was probably chance
it was on my way

---

*Jonas had gone home on his own from a summer party in the neighbor-
hood where the family lives. When he suddenly realized that Jonas was
missing, Birger lost control completely and hit himself until he bled.

†On July 7, Birger ran away from home for the third (and so far the last)
time. At four in the afternoon he suddenly disappeared, leaving the front
door open. He went on public transport over half of Berlin, with his
parents and the police looking for him. Just before midnight the police
picked him up on the Berlin urban freeway (the Avus). That evening and the
next he gave an account of his experiences.

it was only afterwards everything got difficult
the fact is it was very hard to find the way home
really it was quite fun but very very agitating
but it was lets say the only way i knew it was so bad i will never do
it again
lets say east west homes always best

7.7.1991

i am learning really valuable things like what a dangerous
adventure is like
i will do it again but only when its okay
that means first when the kidstuff writing works properly
and second when our fabulous jonas
is bigger and not so worried about our fabulous birger
it upsets a person who can talk when he is worried about
someone
in the first place i am a little sorry about you but not very
much in the second place i need
to be independent
it gets me so worked up when its dangerous
but it isnt as bad as the anxiety otherwise it is much
simpler to run away than being shut up
i am shut up even at home and i can only go out when you
want and never when i want so
how come you are talking about shutting me up when i
always am anyway
dont talk about the freeway
it upsets me so much because it was so horrible
i climbed over the fence that is standing there and i
balanced on it

7.8.1991

most of all i would like to weep like socalled important people
but its no good it is as if a stone being is holding me prisoner and
it thinks sorrow is a security risk it is like an iron ring around
my chest

7.24.1991

how does an important citizen of the world learn to find
the wide expanses if hes never been
where he wants to go

7.26.1991

i create real chaos like a volcano a strong effective will is enough
to quench it there is a surging hasty spirit working eagerly in
me trying to keep the unripe fruits of a person like knowing
lonely genuine steely birger from ripening i want to stop the yield
is too poor

8.20.1991

but iron will isnt enough to destroy addiction i will really
only be free a person like me will change the lonely girl
will be surprised to see how this judgment on me a steely
socalled really stupid person goes
the lonely girl is a socalled crazy girl who came to the
one and only school center today*
everyone there is lonely
simply every autistic is lonely
it does very lonely really severe damage
when they talk properly
these lonely people are so set in their ways
they hide their loneliness
enduring isolation resolutely is difficult
but strange to say you get used to it
in the first place the lonely girl has no real important
confused name how could she get a name
but today she will be much lonelier than me
this poor crazy girl whom lonely rich really stupid birger
quietly loves

9.9.1991

how come birger is so alone again
he changes too slowly

---

*Xenia, a speaking autistic, three years younger than Birger, who had just
  come to the Center.

nobody notices it
unfortunately no one appreciates how difficult it is to turn
    asocial into social behavior
resolutely turn nonsense into sense
changing takes more energy than you really understand
people expect it to take place any time
but nobody asks how difficult it is
i am a coward i am keen to be really successful some time

10.6.1991

but how will calm feel if peace comes to an ever restless person
some day
happens would be a better word
there will just be a quietness in me such as ive never really felt
today i was simply a steely crazy person a lonely person
who just doesnt do what a socially adapted person does these days
its a misfortune for humanity
yesterday it happened in the school center it was because a lonely
crazy birger was irritated by important teachers
an example of how they annoy me is that they just talk on and on
in front of me as if i was air
i seize the first socalled opportunity to interrupt them and i
scream bloody murder
how that happened today i dont know myself
once you said a lonely person thinks up his own way
but i am not thinking at all in that situation

10.10.1991

why do you make such a good meal when so much always makes
you gobble
nobody can go in for all that crazy chewing without consequences

11.5.1991

however for annoying reasons
i will forget all the things ive learned because i say things
which make other autistics envious
because i am giving away secrets that is the trouble

we cannot be saved
we dont want it
i am a real traitor
i will talk and then survive you in eternal safety
a person like me will reap the fruits of my writing some time
its true
i just want to talk a lot
because i simply cannot stand parts of life
you try to convey to me things you feel sure of
but i cant move about properly in society without real terror
reactions

so i get on your nerves too
peace and quiet really get me worked up
because crazy fast thinking begins and goes on for hours
exhausting me
talking relieves it
getting some system into things
its a relief which just seems important i think
a single sentence means
i can find peace where i never ever did before
every terror reaction has its troublesome reason
in a chaos of thoughts
there isnt any other explanation
we watch we are lonely and miles away from important society
a picked bunch of crazy people
like a fractious audience
ruining a fine performance
one day i will tell you all about it
in every detail without bothering about hurting other people
like autistics who want to stay that way because its more comfortable

11.22.1991

i am doing so many stupid things again like never before and i
myself dont know why a strong will fails i cant manage to control
myself all the people in the center are angry with me and keep
scolding me its a catastrophe a thousand times over i give that idiotic team the same trouble

12.9.1991

rustling* is stereotypical behavior which is really intoxicating i am
only doing visibly what loneliness does invisibly

12.26.1991

its a fabulous idea to reduce the cause of autism to a problem which
is almost simple like hearing theres oversensitivity in all areas i can
hear and see a little too much but the sensory organs are okay its just
that theres confusion inside unfortunately words sentences ideas

---

* Running his marbles through his fingers.

get torn apart and torn to bits the simplest things are wrenched out
of the context of the real important single other outside world an
idea is as difficult as a real box of the internal world

1.12.1992

it is nonsense making simple mental problems out of important
questions the way gisela does she is working on the theory that anxiety is a flaw in the mind but anxiety is something which cant be
grasped so easily it is a disturbance i am afraid it is so strong that i
cant describe it my autistic behavior gives an impression of it for instance screaming and biting and all the other senseless things

1.14.1992

why does gisela write to me i dont know her at all and i am sure she
doesnt know how bad i am simply acting as if i didnt have any hand-
icap it is a real deception

1.24.1992

the frightening question is can a socalled autistic loner really make
such a terribly difficult busy choice and in fact destroy buckets of
material all nonsense and garbage
a fabulous important step is surely putting aside seadevils i mean
socalled subconscious things to be worked out at length some day
in torment for a socalled deepsea explorer of the mind

1.26.1992

are you sorry you ever brought confused idiotic totally crazy birger
into this important world

1.31.1992

did you know that squealing cars hurt my ears and did you know
how it hurts when a control mechanism of microphones simply
goes wrong and other noises hurt me too making the wretched conversations of the teachers and other real chosen people all into one
sound they talk so busily and it is all confused
the volume and the confusion are dreadful

2.6.1992

i think even the look in the eyes is part of a persons character
you are often lovingly eager to see rough words
but your eyes look bad
only little jonas is really always kind
in the future i will take a good look at how people cast their secret glances
once in the subway i saw a woman looking at me kindly
it was so nice i often think of it i like to believe in it and i wont forget it
but many looks are hard to bear and bring dreadful suffering with them

2.9.1992

do you use pet names when i am unusually nice or when you are sick of the whole stupid nonsense
how come you love me anyway

2.21.1992

did you know that i am having ideas again for proper reasons
i cant talk to anybody about them in advance
because they have to mature
you ought to give me more recognition i cant do anything else
i have neanderthal neotendencies i am so chaotic today

3.10.1992

for important reasons i can find safety only in the things that people find incalculable and that seem monstrous
i think its infantile the idea we autistics are bushmen and totally chaotic inside
that is only how it looks from outside
inside we are grown up and efficient
even without language we creatures who live in boxes can understand all the nonsense that is said

3.19.1992

the eye examination is to find out
if i see too much
my eyes often hurt
and i see everything it is very hard to bear

inside me i can simply switch it off
and within seconds
all i see is a high wall of dots

3.23.1992

it is nonsense the idea that diet is the cause of similar important obviously autistic symptoms a great part is played by a huge sensitivity of all the senses it cant be cured by any crazy methods built on the idea of a sudden recovery i think we must give ourselves plenty of time and experiment patiently in all areas i will do everything i can to get out of my dog kennel and by that i mean to leave the socalled crate withoutme world

3.25.1992

really losing yourself in things going far beyond the known shore is something i can do too but then a return to the ordinary world seems terribly oppressive i need a long time to find my way to functioning as best i can and for important reasons there are various things i cant express yet the way they ought to be expressed to find out the main causes of autism
i want to stop now because we are just fooling around in the outer suburbs of lousy autism but right there in the middle it is all so dark nobody can imagine it

3.27.1992

right out of those great lectures on poets i would like the one about love poetry in the renaissance* a silly amusing subject keen for action but birger is like that it is tall strong lonely art but very erotic that kind of love thats why i would like to choose the task of picking a specially chosen lecture plain linguistics is boring

3.28.1992

Question: WHY ARE YOU SO RESTLESS?
its just sadness about my condition

---

*Birger is picking the lecture he wanted to attend for his first visit to the university.

the way i keep feeling it
i keep not being able to stand things
and i want to change over to ordinary simple normal life
i just cant even do the simplest obvious things any baby can

4.11.1992

its nonsense to say i am a sour sort of person
i like to have fun
Question: WHAT ABOUT THE APPOINTMENT WITH THE
PHOTOGRAPHER FROM THE MAGAZINE TOMORROW?
i am sure i will be worked up but i will try hard
Question: WHAT WILL GIVE YOU DIFFICULTY?
i cant answer that sweet little rather silly question

5.15.1992

i love language more than anything
it links people
a language gives us dignity and individuality
i am not without language

6.26.1992

its nonsense asking god to help me
a god who makes autistics cant keep on punishing such horrible
people in a spirit of love all the time
however an autistic is always under fire
in particular he cant just accept other peoples hymns of praise
so then he is punished three times over
he is anxious because he thinks that cant be right
such a declaration seems monstrous to me
then he thinks i must hide myself better so that no one will
recognize me
i must deceive everyone so they wont notice me quivering with
FEAR

7.3.1992

itts nonssence that i am crazy
but ii want out of the out of this extraordinary place
remember that

i cant stand the ttalking any more i am crazy even dankward says so
i cannnt hope an y more
iii despaire of myself
i will ne ver be better because my angsiety forcces wont be
how come you think i willl be cured
wwont you give it up
someone like dankward cantt stand it
just a superstition
i can bbe lovable apart from you how come lllove such a perrson
are such moments of encouragement
thank you
i want to stop

7.29.1992
(in the afternoon, after a screaming fit)

terror is the only pleasure i know
so i particularly like the medieval festival*
i fitted in well there
however sympathetic i am i have shouted at people
i am a dark medieval figure

8.8.1992

today i am going to try describing a small incident
we were going by car to mölln to visit my grandma
i was trying hard as usual to breathe quietly and not to rock
and i didnt want to scream either
then suddenly for a moment i saw a very great danger in the form
of a truck racing toward us
i was very scared and i screamed but nobody had even noticed the
danger
in any case this incident shows me that my perception of things obviously works differently
i want to try investigating the differences with other examples

8.18.1992

---

* A medieval festival was being held in Potsdamer Platz, Berlin.

159

why am i obviously restless again
afraid of everything even schwarzenbek*
i would like to retreat into my inner silence i would be glad of it
that way my internal mind would not develop
and i would be a top dropout
i am a terror to you and to me i am a serenade singer without a soul

8.21.1992

which would you rather
for me not to live without help and stay handicapped
or for me to become independent
if so you must just demand more from me
for instance if we go to the store i want to pay by myself
nonsense i am too stupid
once i went out to eat and didnt know how you pay
its only now i realize how little i understand about ordinary everyday life
Question: WHY ARE YOU BITING YOURSELF?
dont do anything that would hurt me
for instance sending me to a home†
dont talk reasonably i am afraid
i want to know if we are going away
i am acting obsessively because today i heard i was going to a
home among other autistics for always
and i will be buried there totally alone
i long more than ever to live without help
i will do anything for that
i am ready to say goodbye to autism
i will murder it

9.23.1992

everything is possible to a real autistic
because of effects arising from unknown reasons
we dont know any bounds

---

* The continuation of his music therapy.

† Birger has misunderstood a conversation between his parents and is afraid
   he will be sent to a home.

an autistic jumps hushabye baby out of his skin
and hushabye baby under his skin

11.4.1992

i have been thrown out of the institution again
because they all say i didnt know what i wanted
because yet again nothing new would go right
Question: WHAT WOULD YOU LIKE FOR CHRISTMAS?
i would like a good edition of crazy nietzsche

11.29.1992

how does it look when i scream
people seem very upset and confused
how come the reactions are so bad
i dont by any means feel all the bad things i see on their agitated
faces
i feel cast out by some bitter mistake
for in their faces i see
they would like to scream themselves scream for rage and fear
and bafflement
the difference is
they darent hurt normal people
and bring confusion to the sad ordinary everyday world
but i am not hurting anyone when i scream
and i need to do it so much to get my balance
perhaps one day i wont always need it but now i am sure it is still
important

12.11.1992

i will ruin myself first and then you
partly on purpose partly for no good reason
i feel bad and i would like to be good
but the evil always gets the upper hand
i am destroying our lives for no reason
again its just a question of venturing on a new beginning
i will have another shot at evaluating what happened today

i will make my way back groping from the world where i am beside myself
i am always discovering ways i have looked for islands
whose shores i guess at
i would be lying
if i were to describe loneliness
as if it were something i wanted
loneliness is my enemy
and i will fight the good fight against it

12.13.1992

Translated from the German by Anthea Bell

The Room

What had made the reflection? It would have had to be some horizontal surface, for the most important aspect of the room was that it was inverted and there could not be a mirror otherwise placed than on the horizontal to effect that inversion.

For he remembered the floor in that other room, from which the chandelier stood straight up, pointing at the ceiling; and the doors whose jambs were three feet tall and whose doorknobs came on the high end, and the two sconces near the floor, and his fantasy: stepping through the little mirror—which suggested a ship's hatch—into the better room.

Then was there some adventure with pirates?

There must have been, else why the hatch?

Perhaps they were pursuing him and the only safety lay in that room.

But could they follow? If they could, was it not likely that his stature and his wiles would allow him to defeat them there?

How could they operate, large and dull, in that close, inverted, foreign room, who'd never seen, nor even dreamed of the existence of the like?

It was in fact, was it not, the only room of the house fitted for him—rightly constructed to offer refuge and accommodation for someone his age.

And all he had to do was procure that reflection on the horizontal surface, then the far room would invert, and show itself ready for him.

On the horizontal surface—but what had that surface been?

A mirrored vanity-table top, perhaps?

Had there been one there? And would it not have held, undoubtedly, a tissue box, a powder puff, the folded guest towels of the Fifties?

Yes, of course.

Had he, then, removed them to make the top clear?

Could he have been that foolhardy—we could not call it courage—would he have been fool enough to so invite his mother's wrath?

But what else could there have been?

There had to have been that horizontal surface; and, explainable by no other hypothesis, it must have been the vanity.

He saw for a moment a small table affair, an étagère, or cart, perhaps, made of brass tubing and with mirrored shelves.

But was that not the drink cart in the living room? It must have been the drink cart which he saw, for the drink cart was as described.

No. As he thought, it came clear to him. It was not the drink cart, but it was a table, perhaps of the same line of design: mirrored shelves, brass tubing, some form of an open table, a conch shell holding balls of soap, the inviolate guest towels in echelon, and, on the shelf below, the tissue box. It must have been, it was; and, in fact, he had braved that wrath and locked the door, and removed the mentioned articles, and placed them—where? Perhaps his fool heart even gave him strength to lay them on the floor, and he procured the horizontal inversion, and down was up in the other room, which functioned as his refuge from the pirates.

How could they best him there? They could not. Could they even follow? The question was open. But, no, he thought not. He thought that a return-to-alignment of the mirrors closed the way into the other room. In fact it seemed to him that he had practiced it, that he had practiced, in his ingress, pulling the medicine cabinet door shut, to erase the existence of the other room. Which, being so, it must, to begin with, have been open.

As it was. It required that alignment between the angle of the mirrored medicine cabinet door and the top of the table, that precise alignment which and only which opened the way. He could almost recall the moment he discovered it.

And now it was his again.

And, so, the drill of replacing the objects—from the floor back to the tabletop in perfect position—had served a double purpose, it had avoided calling down his mother's wrath, and it had perfectly camouflaged his path of retreat from the pursuers.

The secretary said, "He will be with you in a moment," and lowered the phone.

He put the magazines down.

Why had he thought of the room?

Because the man he waited to see was reported to have built a "safe room" inside his home.

This "safe room" was designed to be a refuge in an emergency. He could repair there, bolt the doors, and summon help.

This "safe room"—many in town had had them built—offered protection from the burglar and the assassin.

The doors were generally designed to swing shut instantly, and were made of steel sheathed in wood, and fitted with large and secure bolts. The safe room was designed with its own power supply, and its own telephone line. All one had to do was gain access and one had foiled the intruder's plans.

The fad had swept the town, like any new toy, cherished for its price and for its implication of the buyer's status.

But the man for whom he waited had gone them one better.

Having built the safe room he enjoyed its security only until the question occurred to him: what if the intruder preceded one there? What if he had, by plan or chance, entered the room and somehow caused the alarm which sent the homeowner hurrying into his clutches?

And, so, the man caused a second safe room to be built inside the first.

But the boy had known, he saw now, that the pirates would not follow him into that other world. There he would not be forced to test himself against those stronger or larger than he.

They could not find him there. That accident, that arrangement of mirrors was a coincidence so astronomically unlikely to be duplicated that the boy himself needed both time and luck to bring the other world into being.

"He can see you now," the secretary said.

He put his magazine down and rose from the couch in the gray room.

"Thank you," he said.

No, the pirates were fools, he thought, to think they could frighten me.

And again, they were not fools, they were playmates, chosen for their inability to locate me.

They never wished me ill.

Dummies, Flowers, and Alters

Dummies, Flowers, and Alters

Some of the following installations were accompanied by recorded voice-overs, excerpts from which appear below:

MMPI*, p.170:
As a youngster, I was suspended one or more times for cutting up.
Everything is turning out just like the prophets of the Bible said it would.
I do not read every editorial in the newspaper everyday.
I have no difficulty in starting or holding my bowel movement.
I loved my father.
I am easily awakened by noise.
I like to read newspaper articles on crime.
I enjoy detective or mystery stories.
I have diarrhea once a month or more.
My father was a good man.

Getaway #2, p.171:
What are you looking at? Get out of here! Get away from me. I'll kick your ass. Get out of my face.

White Trash/Phobic, pp.172–73:
WHITE TRASH: (Look into the camera . . . we see you, we see you). (Who's there? Who's there?) The camera sees a suburban sprawl— it's a helicopter shot. And we slowly are through the air and we (away in the sky) can see swimming pools and rooftops and eucalyptus trees and cactus (automobiles), a tennis court and kids on bicycles (airplanes). The camera moves closer and closer to our cul-de-sac (split level). The camera floats down gently to the second story of the house and it begins to drift around. We see some dark rooms and some rooms are lighted. We cannot hear anything. We hear only muffled sounds coming from the interior: a television or a radio, voices talking in a fragmented, (fighting) angry fashion. Then, we hear footsteps, crashing, the voices rise higher, screaming now, (a gun . . . fires). Violence. We can hear them wailing (running).

---

* The Minneapolis Multi-Phasic Personality Inventory. The dummy in this work is responding to a series of questions devised as a diagnostic index for mental illness.

P.O.V. (Point of View), 1993–1994

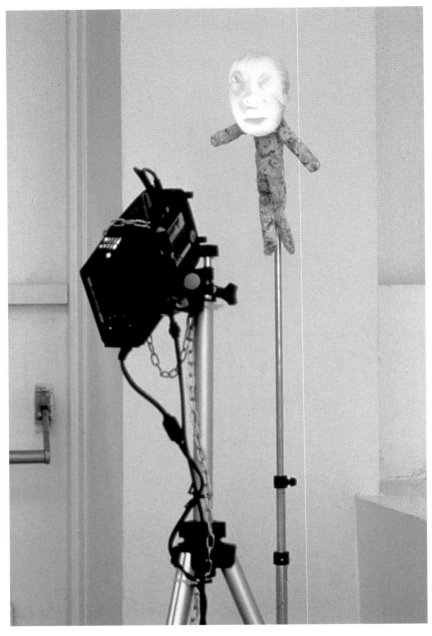

MMPI, 1994

Getaway #2, 1994

White Trash, 1994

White Trash/Phobic, 1994

Phobic, 1994

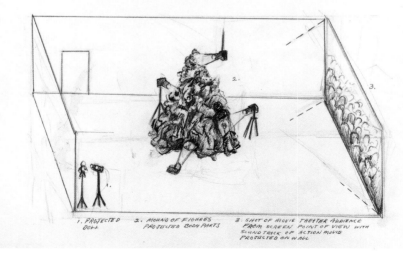

Top: *System for Dramatic Feedback*, 1994
Bottom: *Untitled*, sketch for *System for Dramatic Feedback*, 1994

Movie Block (Sony), 1994

Flowers, 1994

We hear a loud thud followed by a moan and then the crack of hands striking flesh. More footsteps. We see shadows running, cast across the darkened room as figures move past the doors (yelling). A silhouette—someone has just entered the room (blood). (The camera moves in, the camera cannot hide). Cut.

PHOBIC: Imagine you're in a snowsuit or a stroller and you can't move your arms and that you're uncontrollably screaming because you're bound in. Perhaps you're out in the snow and you're up to your knees or up to your waist in snow, and you can't move. And your arms are weighted down, and you're screaming. And perhaps you're in a playpen and it's crowded. And you're weighted down in blankets and you can't move and you're screaming and screaming until you hyperventilate. And you can't move. And you're screaming. Screaming and screaming until you pass out.

Now, there's a group of fellows and they like to dig. And the digger of the group likes to dig down as deep as you are tall. And you enjoy crawling into the hole: it feels good to be in the cool, dark earth. But then the hole collapses, and you're buried in the hole and only your head is sticking out above the ground, and the rest of you is held, compressed in by the earth. And you can't move and all the fellows are laughing and pointing at your head sitting on top of the ground and they won't dig you out. So you're stuck and you're stuck and you're screaming and screaming, "Dig me out of this hole!" And they won't. And then they dig you out.

Flowers, p.176:
I love . . . FUCK YOU! I said I LOVE YOU! I'm going to turn you into the floor. I want you to be the floor. Fuck you. Fuck you. I love you. I love you. You stupid shit . . . Stupid shit. Get to work. Get to work. I said, get to work! Aah . . . uh . . . GET TO WORK! Get to work, you fucking son of a bitch. (Laugh) Uhh . . . uhh . . . You have nothing to say about it. (Laugh) You have nothing to say about it. I'm gonna take you over. I'm gonna kill you. I'm gonna chop yer arms and legs off. I'm gonna kill you.

The Town of Luck

Hedê Kovályové a Praze

Igor told me that when the telephone call came, he was just staring out to sea. There was a small, sharp, triangular squall out on the Adriatic, a sudden dark patch by a lone sail on the near horizon; the boat was riding through the storm in a straight line, undisturbed. In his ear, an impersonal voice from far away announced, without details, the death of the seventeen-year-old son of Viktor Popovic, the Vice President of the Academy. The call was flat and brutal.

He had a seventeen-year-old son himself and the two boys were good friends.

Naturally, he sought explanations. Some things were hard to understand. The young had much to live for. They were not condemned by their pasts; they might even see change. Why did they have to die?

The anonymous voice said, "I believe George Popovic was a friend of your son's. We shall be wanting to ask him a few questions. Do you know where he is? Is he with you?"

Igor said Matej wasn't and he didn't know where he was. Then he walked down the path of rubble to the sea and sat there on the dark pebbles and stared out at the wind on the sea and the boat, immune, moving across the horizon.

It was the sort of anonymous voice that he had long learned

one did not answer. The questions that sort of voice asked simply had no answers.

"You understand," he told me, "I didn't know what had happened. I looked for explanations. I had begun to see that Matej and his friends lived special lives, so they were going to have special deaths."

He had started thinking this way in the summer of 1965, two years before, when he had first heard of the "Night Club," to which many of his son's friends belonged, and began to feel this fear about Matej.

How much, he wondered, had the events of that summer by the lake put a strain on the young of the town of L——? He, as Secretary to the Academy, had been busy organizing the P.E.N. International writers' congress, the first in Eastern Europe since the Thirties. It had weighed on him.

Perhaps the meeting had weighed more than anyone thought on the young? It had certainly been a great strain on Matej: to live for weeks among the complex issues and histories of war and its aftermath that until then had been no more than tales his father told.

The boy, then fifteen, in love with the world but diffident, gawky, slept in the garret of the villa that belonged to the Writers Union. Daily he went off shopping on his bicycle. He helped everyone. And everyone was strange and foreign. Though the guests in the villa all loved Matej, he had not readily admitted their love, or even their admiration. His was a rational mind, in love with astronomy, numbers, gravity, perfection. One did not become intimate with Matej, any more than with the stars and distant bodies.

He came down in the morning and did what needed doing—made the coffee, cut the bread, laid out the jams—with an expression that said to his father: the people here are your kind of people, fanciful people; I'm different; I love you but I'm not of your kind.

Matej and George Popovic were good friends. Igor had a clear image of George: short, curly-haired, fun-loving, a fierce football player in the narrow hallways of his father's large house on Ulyanova Street. When he came to Igor's house to play or study with Matej, Igor took it as a sign that the sins of fathers are not visited on their children.

Unlike Matej, George, Viktor's son, was a member of the privileged class. The fathers of most of Matej's friends had large houses in town. They had large cars. They traveled. Matej's childhood had been different. After the death of Matej's mother (of an infection, not long after the boy's birth), father and son had spent much of their life together reading between the lines that officials like Viktor wrote. There were also those long years, after Igor got out of jail in 1953, when Viktor crossed the street to avoid him.

But by 1965, wasn't that mostly healed? The young men of L— had come in droves to the congress. The local paper had talked of little else for weeks. The young men were enthusiastic: there was wind in their dusty streets and caviar on the tables, there were writers, and hostesses to flirt with.

No doubt Matej had invited George to join him by the lake, and Viktor had probably told his son, "Don't go. It's not a good idea." There were risks to being involved in complex matters.

But Igor did remember that, in the last of the summer nights during those weeks of hope, Matej was often to be found perched on the windowsill of his attic room: with binoculars, studying the movements of birds nesting. Because a pall over father and son there was, both were experts at solitary games.

On one such night, they had rowed out on the lake, whose waters were very still, very dark, Matej leaning effortlessly on his oars, both grace and concentration in his rowing, and behind them, the band of the Grand Hotel playing for the congress's inaugural dance. In the stern of the boat sat two not-so-young lovers, holding hands: he Italian, she English. Igor, ever theatrical, thought to "marry" them. He took them up by the statue of the Virgin in front of the ancient church. Green and phosphorescent, the stones shone even in the new moon, as did the cupola, from which Matej, leaning, lithe, on a rope, rang a bell that echoed over the lake.

It was a metaphorical ceremony. The congress was about marrying East and West: this marriage was an extension of the other. Locally, marriages of convenience were favored over love-matches.

The castle rose to Igor's left; its many-colored lights extended down to the town below. On the return journey, he imagined himself dressed in the peaked cap and diamond patches of the harlequin. Invisible to the world below, he saw himself (the playwright) advancing gingerly along that line of lights, its bulbs, red, green, blue, crackling under his slippers. The line declined steeply. Halfway down came his culminating moment. He reached into his costume and plucked out his heart. He showed it to the crowd below; he made gestures as if to toss it to them. Looking up, he saw behind him the platform from which he had set out. There sat Viktor Popovic, a cautious man, laden with honors and privileges by the state. Popovic wagged a finger at Igor, as if to say, we told you not to. . . . Down below, he felt enmity growl, the groundlings, Americans among them.

He held his heart in his hand, not pulsating, not pumping. It was a satin heart, with frills, yet able to draw the breath out of his lungs, to push him into a long fall, through a wind that lunged at him and thrust him sideways like a sail. Then mysteriously, though there was no applause—not even a murmur anymore from below, wait a minute, there was no one left below!—he found himself seated on a chair next to Viktor on the platform, far above the castle's battlements . . . .

Once they had docked in the boathouse belonging to the Writers Union and left the lovers walking hand-in-hand to the villa, he and Matej walked to the Grand Hotel and peered through the curtains of the ballroom. There they saw David (a grand figure, P.E.N.'s International Secretary) dancing with the Belgian poetess (an amateur) Madame de Geignault. Madame was tall and rigid in his arms; her glasses sloped down her nose while David, florid, English, cut his capers like a contestant on *Come Dancing*.

It was yet another wedding taking place, Igor said excitedly. Matej's arm was draped casually about his shoulder. He took him by the waist and they danced on the lawn in the light that shone through the ballroom windows. "Ssh," Igor said, putting a finger to Matej's lips and dancing him back to the windows. "You see?"

There were five Russians sitting on identical wooden chairs against the wall. One of them (Breitbourd, a Union hack) had prominent gold teeth. The only real Russian writer, old Donskoi, was not there.

It was there, in Matej's room in the Writers Union villa—while Matej and his friends had the run of the lake, the castle, and the high, bare mountains behind—that Igor held his *séances d'amour*. To that room he brought (she might have been the only one, but perhaps not) the woman who had arrived with Tuwim. Her name was Eleanor and

Tuwim was an American writer and critic Igor had met in Berlin in '61 or '62.

Americans fascinated Igor: they were and could be both so fierce and so safe. Igor had invited them both to the villa, along with a Pole (Tadeusz) and the Italian and his English girlfriend (Priscilla).

Eleanor had come to none of the griefs Igor knew. She said simply, "We don't like to belong to anyone." He laughed and said, "We're used to belonging after four hundred years under the Turks." That was after they had made love and she had risen, tall and red-haired, to lean out the window and touch the tree Matej had been climbing for years.

What had happened to that simplicity? Everything that had seemed to open up at the lake had shut down soon thereafter, in the aftermath. Igor had been called to account for his excesses, by Viktor Popovic, among others.

The congress came to a sudden end. Or was it that he had not been paying attention? One night, told by Viktor to see them off, he had driven to the station in the town of L— and watched the Russians stand on the platform, waiting for their train. He had heard their locomotive puff away from the station, catching, as a last image, the sight of Breitbourd's gold teeth behind his hand waving goodbye.

•

O n the afternoon he heard of George's death—no how, why, or when—Igor took the bus from the sea back to the town of L—, a pitiful bag of provisions in the rack above him: a scrawny chicken, four fresh onions. Like the slow journey up over the hills, like the dust that rose about them and eddied in their wake, like the haze that settled on his mind, the death of Viktor's son weighed on him. What if it had been Matej? Matej was his last, his only, attachment. He felt deep pity for Viktor.

In the darkness as they arrived, the window of the bus reflected Igor's face. It was much like his son's. The hair was white and short, brushed forward. The eyes had once been peasant eyes, gray, shrewd like Matej's. Now they were kept invisible by blue-tinted glasses. The mouth was soft, the lips delicately full. His face had been remade, he sometimes thought, by parenthood. In the way bodies took on the taint of their vices, lechery, gluttony, his had taken on softness: breasts, hips, contours, delicacy. But his senses had sharpened with age: ears to hear with, a nose to sniff.

He did not get back to L— until just before dark. He walked home. The chicken in his bag had already acquired a faint odor. As he turned the key in the door, he heard steps within. Then Matej flung the door open. He was radiant. He shone. For what reason? He hugged his father, took the bag from his hand. "We have some tea from England," he said. "Shall I make you some?" The tea came from Priscilla, fair, warm, freckled, the woman he had "married" on the island in the lake. In places like the town of L—, the receipt of tea counted. It meant one existed somewhere else.

In the kitchen, which was tiny, Matej stood leaning against the stove while the water heated, stroking a black kitten. His son was in an excitable, even ecstatic, state, as if suffering from an attack of *petit mal.* Igor found it impossible to ask about Viktor's son George, and Matej didn't mention him. Perhaps he had dreamed that telephone call by the sea. No one had called. George was alive. The police lied to torment him. How else could Matej's smile be so fond when it seemed even the simplest things were difficult to say to each other?

Tomorrow morning, thought Igor, I shall call Viktor. Or I can go by the Academy. Or I will read about it in the newspaper. "Did you buy a newspaper today?" he asked.

Smiling, Matej went to get it, folded neatly by Igor's bed. He said, "Is this what you wanted to see?"

The paper, open to the fifth page, now lay open on the kitchen table. Igor sought out his son's eyes. They were serene. "I had a telephone call yesterday," Igor said. "That's why I came back."

"Yes, I know. From the police."

"They were looking for you."

"They were here too."

"Why were they looking for you?" Quite without his willing it, Igor's eyes strayed down the page. He made an effort not to look. "What did you say to them?"

"I said I knew what they wanted."

"What did they want?"

"To know about George."

"What did you tell them?"

"I said I knew all about it. They said, 'Tell us.'"

"Yes, and what did you tell them?"

"Nothing. That's what you told me to do. You taught me never to tell the police anything."

"If you didn't tell them and you know everything, why don't you tell me?"

The kitten leaped out of Matej's arms and scampered down the hall, with Matej following.

Automatically, Igor's eyes buried themselves in the paper. He read, not just once, but several times, the few lines on the fifth page, neatly underlined with the ruler which, meticulous with possessions, Matej had kept since his father had fetched him from school the day he came out of prison.

"George Popovic, aged seventeen, a first-year student at the L— Polytechnic Institute, was found dead yesterday evening at his home, Ul. Ulyanova 18."

What could one make of this death? It was senseless, unearned. He imagined finding Matej dead. He thought of Viktor and how he must feel. For all their differences, he too had an only son. "There are a lot of families in the town of L— who have but one child," he had said to Tuwim during the conference. "After the war we didn't want to take any risks, we didn't believe in posterity."

Igor had been much taken with Tuwim; he loved the warthog in him, the bristling savagery, his scarce hairs, the tufts of red on his scalp. "Listen, Igor," Tuwim said during the meetings, "I don't understand the games here. Is Viktor your friend? He doesn't seem to be very supportive." Igor tried to explain: well, the nature of friendships was obscure. In this part of the world. That is, you couldn't count on friendships. "Even in the worst times, when Viktor felt compelled to cross the street so as not to meet me on the sidewalk, he still kept in touch. You understand? I'd get brief, ambivalent telephone calls, he'd leave unsigned notes on my desk." Igor had been expelled from the society of people like Viktor. But still he was wanted. That was the way things were here. When God expelled Lucifer, was it really forever? "We are children of the same revolution," Igor said. "We cling to a common past. But what if we were *all* wrong?"

How was an American to understand? Tuwim's mouth snapped

like a turtle's—on less good teeth. Igor already figured in the book Tuwim was writing about the "other" Europe. But he had not made up his mind about him. He wanted to spring him into everyone's mind, so to speak, *in medias res.* "Yes sir, he opened his fly and pissed eastward on a cold night: one drunk, unhappy Slav." He embraced Igor clumsily. Igor was his dissident in this country, but he found him ambiguous.

Igor shrugged and said to Eleanor: "Your Tuwim's another chorus." He told her about the Russians sitting along the edge of the wall in the ballroom. That was their role, he explained. They were the chorus. They commented on his life, as they had been commenting on his life and on the lives of all his friends ever since the war. Like all such choruses, they were apparently there forever. And basically, they wanted to correct him.

·

Still, a son was a son. Igor sat in his kitchen trying to make up his mind to call Viktor Popovic. Matej had returned. He was leaning over his father's shoulder, the black kitten was draped about his slender neck. "You've read it," he said, looking down at the paper opened up in front of Igor. "George had his moment of pleasure. Now let's not talk about it any more."

What did the boy mean by that? Igor felt it might be dangerous to say anything to Matej. That mood of intense happiness was still with his son, inhabiting his wide, generous smile, the tender gray of his eyes, the delicacy of his hands on his father's shoulders: like being in love.

Again, Matej escaped. From the door of the basement, Igor caught a glimpse of him going out the garden gate, wearing the night like a cat. Igor himself went to the theater, where his play was in rehearsal.

It was always cold in the unheated theater—a cinema on weekends. The boys, mostly students, were in leotards. The girls stood about the walls in postures stolen from Picasso and Degas postcards. They were of course not girls. Igor's theater had come to being in prison, where there were no women; by maintaining that convention, Igor maintained his prison. By night these girls had the blue hue of beard up above their body stockings and under their goldilocks wigs. Igor's carpenter friend, Marek, doubled as set-builder and character actor. He had come out of prison a year after Igor, showed up at his door, asked only for tools and a roof over his head, and had then built the tiny wooden basement warren in which Igor lived, all joinery, walls that absorbed beds, tables that folded away, spaces to hide, to store, treasure troves. Having finished, he had left without a word.

There was a dog in all of Igor's plays. In this one, *The Firehouse*, the Chief was dressed in a blue policeman's tunic. In a fierce mask, and with a long, demoniacal tail which slapped the floor as he walked, he was a bulldog. The boys (Matej was not among them, but sometimes, in company of his friends or alone, he sat at the back of the long, narrow hall) ran all over the stage putting out fires. They tripped over hoses and pails, struck heroic postures, posed for photographs with their helmets tucked under their arms. The girls leaned out of balconies and begged to be saved. It was a farce in which lovers confronted each other on tall ladders, bodies hurtled into blankets.

The fires were all imaginary. Artificial red flames shone through the cellophane windows of the set. At the end of each mission, the firemen slunk away, ridiculed, out of place and unwanted. None of them understood fires were simply tasks invented by the Chief to keep them on their socialist toes. The board on which he wrote down their quotas with a red marker, big as a salami, was hidden from them. Their firehouse was surrounded by a sea of troubles, literally: waves splashed against the walls, the wind-machine howled. In the last act—the firehouse itself on fire, the arsonist (the Chief himself) slinking away with a last defiant leg raised against a hydrant—the firemen rushed cheerfully into the burning house, overjoyed with their own immolation, cheering the Chief.

This rehearsal was refractory. Igor could detect a sniffing, a dislike, a contentiousness. Franciszek, the Chief, pulled angrily on a cigarette; he showed his hands, chafed by sliding down the fire pole. "I don't know what the matter is," he said. "People are distracted. Artur was slow getting down, he's like an old woman! And don't laugh, Igor, goddamn it! There's nothing to laugh about!"

Was it just nerves? The play wasn't good? The critics were out to bite? They'd had word from the authorities and he, Igor, hadn't heard?

As always, Igor touched his actors. His hands fell like liquid on their shoulders. Thinking of his son, or of the young in general, he exuded more than the usual amount of love. His eyes misted behind his dark blue glasses. That night it was as if some outside wind were blowing through the old cinema. His actors had cold hands. They stared at him expectantly: could he whistle up another play out of thin air? Hadn't he any better words than these? One of them (George) was missing. In a bright pink dress, only Boyan, who had the female lead (he was the Chief's secret mistress), was radiant. Like Matej.

He spent an anxious night, as in prison on the eve of executions. Worn out, he could not fall asleep. Words, phrases, ran through his head. None of them were worth putting on paper. All of them were far too close to his own life.

Sleep had saved him before. At the conclusion of his trial, faced with a row of stern judges, his peers, and standing on a box, Igor had fallen into a delicious sleep. On another occasion, in the mountains, surrounded, with Germans moving through the shadows like Cossacks on stolen horses, firing from the waist into the huddled bodies there, only Igor had survived, motionless, genuinely asleep.

Like Prague or Budapest, L— is a circuitous town. A castle looks down on the lower town. One climbs, in circles, on cobblestones. Igor lived above, in the old town. Early, he wound his way down the hill until he hit the broad avenues below. The Academy was on the 6th of May Avenue. There was a lime tree on either side of the imposing door. The receptionist, stranded alone on an expanse of parquet, had a bowl of pale flowers on her desk. She was an elderly lady, a gentlewoman and a distant cousin of Josip's (the President of the Academy). When Igor asked if Viktor was in, she dabbed at her right eye with an embroidered handkerchief (the funeral had been the day before).

Igor knew Viktor would be there and he went up the marble stairs and into his office. Igor put out his hand. "I was by the sea," he mumbled. "I'm so sorry."

Viktor was a tall, dry man, a historian. It was like addressing a tombstone bearing a withered wreath made of a brown tie and brown silk handkerchief. Igor remembered Josip saying, "You must not be against him because you think he lacks courage. The war took it out of him. Afterwards, he was tortured. Perhaps he was never a brave man, but he convinced himself that he was and so, by the rules of the game, he had to suffer."

"Thank you. I wish I had something to say. I do not understand it. Would you not say George had everything? They have everything, these young people. They didn't have to fight for it; they escaped the worst times. His room is full of LP's. He has American jeans." The historian, obsessed by the abstraction that is time, struggled with the physical fact that is death. Viktor's face was blank, without details. As was so often true, in these parts, the facts of what had actually *happened* were missing. Stories began and were never continued; one didn't dare ask.

"We don't know what they're up to, the young," Viktor continued bitterly (Igor was surprised at this sudden vehemence). "We don't know what they're up to until it's too late. God knows what fool games he and Matej and the rest of them have been playing."

"Is that why the police called?" Igor asked.

"They haven't seen you?"

"No, I told you, I wasn't here. I was by the sea."

"With Matej?"

"No, Matej was here. I think. Was he with George?"

Viktor looked at him peculiarly. "You don't know, do you? Your son hasn't told you." At that moment, Viktor looked swollen with hatred for Matej; his Adam's apple stuck out angrily. Then, just as suddenly, Viktor was as gray as ever. "George hanged himself," he said matter-of-factly. "I thought you would have known. My wife came home and found him." As Viktor spoke, Matej became shadowy.

Blackout. On stage, his son is like Hamlet. He sits on a high stool, his legs crossed, his fine long hands white against the black of his tights, his cropped hair brushed forward. But the idiot boy is grinning. Igor is furious with him. The whole effect of the scene is spoiled.

Hanged? The two men looked at each other. They'd seen men hanged, in the war: they swung gently in the wind, iced, their limbs stiff, their necks askew, their boots stripped.

"Why? How?" Igor heard himself say. "Was it a love affair?" Was George a Bazarov, a nihilist? How could one be a nihilist in this part of the world, in the town of L—? There was no one to overthrow, no tsar to lob bombs at. Just people like Viktor. They had arrived early at nothingness, without a struggle.

Two days passed. No Matej. Viktor had gone out of town. Where was Matej? He thought of the three sisters who stood in a silver frame on Josip's desk: Matej might be there. On his arrival, Olga, the eldest, rose from the sofa in an Italian silk print dress, held out her hand and said, half teasingly, half invitingly: "Igor, you're just what's been missing since Papa went away. You would like tea, of course?" The darling child of socialism rang a silver bell imperiously. He did not even remember them at the lake, though, of course, with their father presiding over the sessions, they must have been present.

"Of course we were there!" said Xenija, the most ravishing and the least settled of the three. "We had the whole Russian delegation, don't you remember? Staying at the Marshall's villa?"

"Of course you did."

"We were an underclass," Valerija smiled. "You didn't pay any attention to us."

"You were young."

"Oh, not so young. We mimeographed, we proofread Papa's speech, we went dancing with the Americans...."

"Was it a good time?" He tried to imagine one of the sisters dancing with Tuwim.

"That's just what we were arguing about."

How long could they sustain their Edwardian drawing room comedy and not see the anxiety that gripped their guest? Or did they talk so prettily to calm him? *Adesso è finita la commedia.* "You must excuse me," Igor said, as the maid brought in the tea (silver service, china cups). "I came with intent." They all looked up together. Intent? "Oh, nothing sinister. I wondered whether you'd seen Matej. He seems to have vanished since last night."

"Another moody one," said Xenija, who was inclined to speak her mind.

"Yes, they are all aflutter," added Olga.

"You knew George."

"He was here. Often. All of them came here."

"But we are not," Olga reminded them, "the *jeunesse dorée* of L—, you know!"

Igor remembered Matej saying, "I know all about it." What was

George's "moment of pleasure"? Did they know? He described the
scene at the theater, and then his day at the sea and the mysterious
anonymous call, even the smile on Matej's face. As he restaged it for
the sisters, he watched their faces for complicity, for knowledge,
intuition. Something, a lot, flickered between them. "Another
moody one, you said. What did you mean?"

Yes, they acknowledged they'd said that. As Olga meticulously
poured out tea they all talked a little, dropping their voices—as
though Mama and Papa might overhear them from Paris. A sort of
fashionable pessimism, they said. The "Night Club." Perhaps he'd
heard of it? "It's all that nonsense at the University," Valerija said.

"It came to a bad end," added Xenija.

"But, Igor, you should understand," said Valerija. "There was an
element of playfulness. It started as something of a joke."

"A joke among *boys*," inserted Olga.

"About fathers. A Turgenev joke."

"Was I included?" asked Igor.

This they considered. No, they didn't think so. They hadn't seen
Matej in a while. "He didn't feel as free coming here. You know, after
the P.E.N. congress," Xenija said. "He'd become a grown-up. We all
felt that a little."

"No, I think it was more people like Papa and Viktor," Olga said.

"Yes, that's right! Who thought that everything was all already
settled," put in Xenija. "Kafka junior would become a cigar mer-
chant like his father. This was the kingdom they would inherit." She
waved a long arm at the table, the tea service.

"But not us," teased Valerija.

"Most certainly not us," her younger sister pouted.

"So," said Igor, "they were in love, these boys, were they? Matej,
George, Boyan, their friends... "

"Oh yes. All the time. In raptures. But it wasn't the real thing. In
love with the idea of love."

"But not frivolous," the sisters chimed in, "no, certainly not
frivolous."

"Then you don't really know all about it," said Igor.

No, they had inklings, there was a brotherhood, there were
adolescent pacts sealed in blood, solemn oaths. That sort of thing.

The police were on his doorstep when Igor got home: two gray men with white caps. There was a hint of autumn in the air, as though they'd brought cold air behind them, but the power to harm had left policemen by now. They knocked patiently, by the light of day; they observed procedures; they wore the same burdened air as their colleagues in other countries.

Igor invited them in. He felt an urge to giggle. These were stage policemen, digging into their satchels, then laying out, smoothing with heavy hands, a primitive copy, carbon paper, blue, near illegible. Did he have any idea who the other signatories of this letter…this letter here…might be?

"The original," the older one said with solemnity, "was signed in human blood."

Igor pushed his glasses up, his eyes swimming. They stared at him, the two of them, and he understood that they were peasants such as he'd known in his village as a boy, marching up the road with immense, sharp scythes swung over their shoulders; they were wood-cutters and mushroom hunters, from his village or even Josip's, the same sort of simple men who'd joined up in the mountains.

But there were deeper currents in them than he had seen. They looked at him half sorrowfully and half forgivingly, like the good Catholics they were: how could he treat all this as a game? He, an educated man: just consider the books in this flat. However small, the atmosphere of a tiny civilization: flowers in a dark blue bowl, a Vermeer reproduction in which the folds of the dress matched the blue of the vase. A secretary to the Academy, whose plays, as their dossiers informed them, odd, heterodox, were performed all over the country; occasionally, even outside. It went to prove, didn't it, that the people with such brains didn't necessarily have their heads screwed on right.

It was the fathers who had sent these men on their errand. Those fathers who had sons, as they now explained patiently. They *had* to check. Every son in George's class at school, and some in classes below. Couldn't Igor see? They were all afraid. These sons, too, could be smiling beatifically, but there was death at the end, and there were beliefs at the beginning.

What beliefs? Well, obviously some that were dangerous. To themselves. That the fathers sensed. The spirits of these boys were not grounded. Not in the state, which gave them everything they could want. "Excuse us, Igor," they said. "We know you've had your ups and downs, but still, you do not live as we do, eh? It's rarer air up there, no?"

"Who, what, is Emöke?" they asked. "It is a Hungarian name, that's all we know."

"Yes," said the other, "We have come simply for your help."

Emöke. Igor knew that name.

A window opened in a hot room, memory, then relief. Through the window he saw Matej and the window shut again.

"Why do you want to know?" he asked the two policemen, suddenly frightened. His soul wore no clothes; a nasty wind blew through his ribs. "You've heard of the 'Night Club'?"

They said—how could he be so stupid?—"But it's there on the paper. It's signed 'Emöke.'"

A week went by. There were more rehearsals. Boyan grew hysterical under the seductions of the Chief, increasingly real. Importuned, ravished, he leapt with ever greater abandon from ladders into blankets. The last act would not work. In the middle, as Igor was rewriting, Matej came back. He had late sun on his face. He'd been dazzled—climbing in the Carinthians. He said he wanted to see them before the sun disappeared.

True enough: autumn was racing in. Wind and rain did nothing to appease Igor. Not even Matej's return did that. He discovered a thirst for his son, a need to feel him near and tangible. He asked Marek to drive them down to the sea. Marek had a Fiat. Who knew how he'd obtained it.

Igor sat up front. He made new connections all the time. For a while, earth, air, fire, and water blended. The sun from Italy across the way was brutal. When they came to the house where Igor had heard the news of the death, it looked abandoned. In a last autumn outburst, weeds had grown up around the door, the fields were unmowed. It was a troubling image: it might have been himself, shuttered, grapes rotting, pecked at by birds.

It didn't seem to bother Matej. He looked with pleasure at the sea where there was no storm at all.

Fear was undefinable. God never said He was offended, but Igor knew and was afraid for no good reason. In Igor's mind, the sea existed to subtract his son from the earth. Also from the town of L—, which represented air: in which George had been swaying when his mother came home one night.

For that reason, nothing was asked about Emöke or pacts signed in blood. If Matej talked about George, it was as George had been throughout his adolescence, the boy with whom he swapped western comic books and science fiction. George came back to life, or had never been dead. Hadn't they climbed the battlements of the castle by the lake together? The last day of the meeting, hadn't they set off the fireworks just when the Chief (the fire chief in Igor's play was the Chairman of the Writers Union in life) was about to speak?

"We were all there, the last day," Matej said. "We had an agreement." Five of them with matches to the fuses. Nothing to do with Emöke.

The first night in the house by the sea (Marek had insisted on going back to L—), Igor found himself counting backward through summers with Matej. In a room lit by a candle. Last summer, where were we? The summer before? And the one before that? All the way back to the first summer Matej could remember. That was the summer Igor had come out of prison.

"I hadn't forgotten you," Matej said. "You were all I thought about."

This didn't mean that father and son loved each other, although they did. It meant they had no choice about love.

The point was, the sea seemed to be working. That ecstatic smile on Matej's face evolved into contentment; he worked steadily at his schoolwork, and was, slightly, in love. With Xenija, Josip's youngest daughter. At a distance, Matej said, with the most pleasant blush. Whatever storm there had been, it had now passed. The boat had returned serenely to harbor. Father and son frolicked on the beach while Igor recited passages from his new last act (it had to be made much plainer that his firemen, rushing into the burning building, were engaged in a collective suicide). Matej read the parts out loud; they played at being actors, with pebbles in their mouths.

When Igor again took the bus back to L— (Matej asked to be left by the sea a while longer to close up the house), it was with the hope that he had mastered both the town and his own fears. But, no sooner was he back, the town of L— presented him with the unexpected, the grotesque. He quickly understood its underlying malevolence.

The town of Luft. Luftstadt. Airtown.

Have I said that Igor was terrified of dogs? It is not the sort of fear that should be left unmentioned, for it belonged to the very old fears. When Igor emerged from prison, he was lodged over the municipal pound. All the dogs in his life were relatives and descendants of the dogs that had been killed below him.

The dogs of L— are not the pampered dogs of Tuwim's New York; nor those, even more fastidious, of Igor's much-loved Paris. They are few; they are largely hungry. Cats L— tolerates. They eat scraps, they curl up in tiny balls to fit small rooms. The citizens of L— make great efforts just to stay alive. Cats accept that.

That afternoon, as Igor headed for yet another rehearsal, he was caught in a dog-pack. One was piebald, with a lopped ear; another black, wet like sealskin; two were grizzled, brown, with matted hair. A wind was blowing horizontally, a wet autumn wind, sawing at the belt of Igor's raincoat. The dogs' muzzles slanted downward at shoelaces and cuffs. They drove him across the street, missing a bus, into a shop door (a few mannequins in the window looked away in disgust) and back across the street again. He kicked at one (people were looking); another he scraped against a wire bin. The black dog glared angrily. The two brown dogs growled.

Pushed this way and that, he found himself by the extinguished neon curlicues of the Kino Eisenstein, his theater, closed for repairs. Why were they suddenly working on it? Had the authorities closed down his play? Outside, a blue light pulsed on a police car. Miraculously, the dogs had stopped at the edge of the crowd, whimpering; now they squatted and cowered.

Igor pushed through the crowd. He was drawn through the double doors from which the familiar old rusty chain still hung. Inside, there were rows of seats covered in dust sheets, an audience of plaster, cavernous dark red walls lit by a single bulb high in the ceiling. His stage had vanished; the firehouse set was hidden by a screen. Things like this happened, he knew, and then unhappened, all in a week. L— was the sort of place where the audience sat stony-faced through comedies directed against the authorities for fear of spies in the audience; the audience itself became a troupe of actors, pretending not to understand.

He sat down and stared about him, wiped his glasses, considered the proscenium arch, his role, his lines, other lines that were forming in his head, a procession of mythological dogs—Cerberus, three-headed guardian of the infernal regions, among them.

"Yes, please, you." He turned around and in the very back, at the top of the long aisle, he saw a man, fat, in a gray greatcoat. In the soft light that fell from the projection booth above him, Igor could make out the sweat on his face; the dog-like anger, too. "Yes, you," the man repeated. "What do you want here?" How was it possible to answer such a question? Igor wasn't there by choice; but also, he couldn't deny that he was there. "What's the matter with you?" the fat man said, coming down the aisle toward him (he had a peculiar, lurching walk, belly to the front, each hip moving its own way, unconnected): "You can't be in here."

At that moment, Igor felt exceedingly tired. There was a workman's tin box on the floor beside him; he saw two cigarette butts on the worn carpet. He fell quickly asleep. He felt his shoulder being shaken. The fat man, barrel-chested or bellied, glared down at him. "You can't sleep here," he said, grasping Igor by his raincoat collar. "Get out of here."

Eventually he was called back to the projection booth in the remoter back of the cinema and Igor followed him. Both drawn and impelled. It was as he had feared when he had first seen the dogs. Crowded by the twin projectors, with little room between the high metal stool (on which he must have stood) and the concrete back wall, they had managed to lay out the young man who had hanged himself from the pipe that ran across the ceiling. Igor recognized him at once as Boyan: by his overbright red lips, the heightened color on his cheeks. Apart from the red-black darkening bruise on his neck, the most noticeable thing about Boyan was the rictus on his face, a silly, incompetent grin, with high spots on his cheeks, as if from embarrassment.

It was Tuwim who had invented one of his dogs for him, the dog of old age, shaggy, smelly, and brown, who was content to sleep and growl, to eat and grow, until slowly, locked in the room which was his own dying, he was able to draw no breath. It seemed so unlike an American story, Igor had insisted. Tuwim, short of breath himself, elaborated: its jaws, the heat of its breath, the loose flaps of its jowls, the gleaming gums, the matted weave of its hair, a prickly blanket, its burrs, its sniffing and snuffling.

This was in Berlin, among the well-bred dogs that dined at the Kempinski along with the best of them, and he'd told Tuwim about coming out of prison, his second prison.

He said blithely—Igor was always blithe, his hands made gestures in the air as his voice made parabolas—"You won't believe me, it's as old Donskoi says, there's no way of imagining what it's like. You see," and his voice dropped confidentially, "it would have been easier if they could prove I was mad, therefore they tried to make me mad. When I got out, and after I went from friend to friend begging for a room, any kind of room, in which I could live with Matej, and each had his excuses, I went to the Housing Bureau and insisted that I had a right to be housed. But I was branded a pervert, an enemy of the people, and for a long time they refused to find me anything. Then one day they offered me a big sort of attic in a stone building in the old town. The roof leaked, there was just a skylight, it was damp. Take it or leave it, they said.

"When I had moved in, they made the part downstairs into the dog-pound. Every day a truck went out and collected all the mutts from the street and brought them to the old stone building. And every morning the dogs who had been there unclaimed for a week were taken out to a yard in back and shot. I could see them from my window.

"We say animals don't know about the future, they have no anticipation. But you can inform them of their fate. That's what I did every night when it got quiet. I put my ears and my mouth to the floorboards and talked to them. I'd talk to them and they'd begin to howl. You know, they're just like us; they don't want to die yet. They growl and bark and whine all night, and what they're saying is, 'Wait a while, we haven't yet understood what life is about, we're not ready, okay?' It didn't do them any good."

It's in Tuwim's book now. All the dogs in L—, Igor said, knew who he was. It was as if he'd never got rid of the stench. He was the death salesman.

Tuwim says that after the second suicide, Boyan's, Igor became a driven man: as though he could save his son by staging his own disasters. He ran from one father to another. Fragments of their anxieties gathered in his mind; those pacts sealed in blood grew firmer, more solid. But always, in the various panics he found, there was another, still voice that said (in the seductive tones of mothers in tailored suits, of fathers who shopped at the special stores and smelled of cologne), my son wouldn't do a thing like that. What possible reason could he have? No, their son was upstairs: listen, they said indulgently, you can hear him, he's playing his records, we brought him back some Beatles! No, Sasha is preparing for his exams. Boris is with Stefana, you know Stefana?

The town of L— was full of denials.

A wall had been built between parents and their children. Sasha and Boris, like George and Boyan, did not come down from their rooms; they did not receive, pour tea, play duets.

The police were interviewing all the members of one class at the university, the morning papers said. There were rumors of an antisocialist plot led by two professors. A letter by Boyan was found in his bedroom. A scandalous incitement, the paper said, refusing to quote it.

At home, Igor ransacked his son's basement room, one whole wall of which was occupied by a painting of his own in startling, even desperate, colors. As though a dog had barked loudly in his ear, Igor jumped. On the shelf before him was the book he remembered Matej showing him. He opened it. It contained a story, *Emöke*: from between whose pages fluttered a piece of tissue paper. Matej, or someone, had used a child's stencil to print, in long, uneven lines, a set of messages:

> *Suicides of the world, unite!*
> *You want a real goal for society, get hanged!*
> *The rope—A better tool for a better life!*

Oh, such raucous boys! Who played such games!

Igor felt as if he were reliving the day he was released from prison and went back to L—. He remembered standing at the wicker gate of Matej's school for a moment, unsure of where he stood with the world (with his shaven head, his reputation), before he walked in and through the first door on his right. It had cloven his heart to see Matej at his little desk. Then to have Matej's three-year-old hand thrust into his own and eyes looking up at him as he explained fiercely how often he had *tried* to rescue him from prison but Auntie wouldn't let him.

Now he found he could no longer breathe. His ribs were

crushed against his back with premonition.

Of course it was in Matej's character to disappear for days. He went hiking in the mountains, he stayed on the floor at friends' houses, girls wrapped themselves around him and blotted out those luminous eyes: Wasn't he the freest of spirits? Wasn't that an agreement between them? Matej had grown up without the worst of games—hide and seek, king of the castle, anything that involved predator and hunted, anything that had the tinge of capture.

But now all that remained of Matej in this apartment was his smile. Igor felt forsaken. It was as the priests said: hell is solitude, it is being abandoned by God. He picked up the book (it was by a Czech writer) and then, feeling terribly sleepy, sat down to read it at the kitchen table. Puss hadn't been fed. She rubbed against his ankles, voiceless, sable black.

It had all sorts of connections, that book, he now remembered. It had come during that summer on the lake. Matej had brought it into the villa after the sisters had borrowed it from Heda Kovály during the congress. As he read, the words in the book seeped into his mind. He didn't entirely absorb them, but they floated through with their own kind of beauty, a beauty that came from somewhere else.

In the tale, there were four characters on a socialist holiday: a lewd and vulgar teacher, a fat woman, a young intellectual, and Emöke, who was tall as a street lamp and aimed toward God. Igor understood that the intellectual in the story was in love with Emöke, yet afraid of loving her. It was a fear she inspired—being spectral. In the end, he lacked the courage to utter his love, which for Emöke meant so much. She was frightened of returning to the carnal world of her husband, to what the writer called her "primal damnation." Igor's finger lay on the passage: *the primal damnation that is the root of her feelings of inferiority and the source of her life-giving force. . . . It is of this damnation that a new human being is born, a child.* The young intellectual was bound to be afraid, wasn't he? Unlike her, he was not made of wind. Emöke vanished. He was left at a remote train station at one in the morning, with a white arm waving to him, *the arm of that girl, that dream, that madness, that truth, Emöke.*

Whom memory effaces. It made sense. She was not unlike death. This book from another country, passed from hand to hand, a forbidden text, had touched the young of L—, grown on them, lodged in their hearts, like lichen.

He fell asleep at the table, then woke up with the anguish still there, a dog that had sunk its teeth into his stomach, was still, then shifted his jaws.

Also, it was opening night. (The Kino Eisenstein was, once again, mysteriously repaired, replastered. The body had been taken away.)

There were fewer people than usual in the audience. It was perhaps the snow. They stamped in in boots. The three sisters carried large umbrellas. Like Graces. But instead of sitting in their usual seats, they clung together in a row near the back, talking to no one.

His actors were restless, like animals. The boy who had taken over Boyan's role was nearly in tears: he couldn't fall in love. Those who were meant to be rustic girls, over-lipsticked and rouged like dolls, spoiled their effects by being impassive. The boys panicked. What took place on stage was real.

In the last act, while the Chief bristled in his dog-body, his tail pointing upwards like an arrow—he had to organize a world that was falling apart—Igor's head exploded. So strong was the anxiety that overtook him that it forced him out of his seat.

He realized Matej had keys to the Writers Union villa. Sometimes he went up there to draw or read. The cold never bothered him. He had his own room on the very top floor, a former maid's room, the room in which Igor had first, and then often, made love to Eleanor. Igor saw the tree up against Matej's window. Winter green.

He ran backstage where Marek was manipulating lights against cellophane filters, making wind stir the flames by blowing through a conical tube. The firemen were about to rush into the building. He grabbed Marek by the arm. "Your car," he shouted through the shouting. "I must have a car!"

The firemen were, it seemed, parents. They sought to save their children from the inferno. The audience, such as it was, rustled like flames. Igor could hear their sibilance. There were gutter-calls, snipings, coughs, a few walkouts, much suppressed anger. They seethed; their children were beyond recall.

He drove from the town of L— into a tunnel of snow. Nothing mattered, least of all death.

Marek dropped him off at the Grand Hotel on the lake, and he remembered watching the bodies dancing, Matej's arm about his shoulder. He and Marek argued and Igor stamped away in the snow.

"You should trust your son. As I trust you," Marek shouted after him.

"I don't trust you," Igor shouted back bitterly.

He went first to the villa, but no light burned inside. It was cold. Running back down the hill, out of breath in the dark rhododendrons, he crossed the strip of light that marked the shore road and stumbled across to the shingled Hapsburg boathouse where the pleasure boat was usually moored—in which he had taken the not-so-young couple to be married. That had been summer; this was autumn, now winter.

It was dark inside, the water so still it reflected the darkness, seamless. The boat was missing. But there was another one, less heavy, that belonged to the president of the Writers Union, his Fire Chief. He stole that boat.

The painter, dropped overboard, slapped loudly on the water. As he'd been taught as a boy, he stood up amidships and pushed against the oars, facing the island church and bell tower, God punish him, wet snow in his face. It grew into eyelashes. Dogs were barking, far out on the water; music started in the hotel ballroom, union hours, down to three players, violin, saxophone, bass fiddle.

When he turned to look back at the little town on the lake, the villa and its tall pine, he saw the castle tower. Matej and George and Boyan had climbed ropes to light the fireworks. They'd come up with their parents because everyone was there: it was the final day. The Chief had been there: not in his dog costume but in a dove gray tunic with sash and medals. Viktor had been there and David had danced with Madame de Geignault. Breitbourd with his gold teeth did a hopak. Peering back through the snow at the castle, *lumière* but no *son* now, he saw Breitbourd again, knees jerking, apoplectic legs in heavy twill kicking out. He looked desperately toward his masters in the Soviet delegation. There stood Donskoi, applauding half-heartedly with one rough hand against another, laughing only at Breitbourd's teeth flashing in the arc lights.

Igor remembered himself, high in the air on his wire, realizing that all these people, assembled as lovers, moved to talk, to wed, would disperse. Miles below him, Don Pablo Neruda had been preparing to return to the Isla Negra, his cookbooks and poems—

Stalin alza, limpia, construye, fortifica,
preserva, mira, protega, alimenta,
pero, también castiga . . .

Ignazio Silone, bullish, had been about to fold into the last years of his life. Donskoi had bid farewell, with his delegation, at the station in the middle of the night. The Americans, the British poets, would return to their safe academies. David would no longer dance with Madame de Geignault. The days of bonhomie would end. The marriage was off.

Igor had looked down tremulously at the audience, thinking how many ways there were to kill oneself. What he had wanted was to float like a leaf down to the sea.

Then, when the new President had closed the conference and given his address, the Chairman of the Writers Union got up to give a farewell speech. He was thick as a bear. His growl had barely started when, from five points, including the tower, the fireworks went off, banging and fizzling among the thick stars. The Chairman's mouth had dropped; not even clichés emerged. And Igor, overtaken by giggles, had fallen asleep.

Here, the sleep was all around him. Snow like feathers from a pillow. Ahead of him in the dark, a bell tolled once.

Here is what Igor wrote about that night. That Matej's body was still warm; that a fabulous hope swooped into his own heart; that he kissed it, to breathe life back into it; that he ran down to the tavern (which was closed, now that the season was over), the same tavern where he and the Italian and the English girl who sent him tea had sat and drunk cool white wine; that he had woken up the couple who ran the tavern and they had come out, he in trousers with suspenders pulled up over his nightshirt, she in a greatcoat; that he had used their telephone, then watched the motorboat, a blue light on its bow, carry a doctor from the opposite shore of the lake.

And that, later, the police came and took photographs but no fingerprints. Still later, men in black came and carried his son's perfect body away in a coffin and he stayed there listening to the gravel creak under heavy boots.

II

As for myself, Eleanor, the situation was this. I had been living with Tuwim in New York for most of the previous year. I was twenty-six, he nearly forty; I, a student, he, a teacher. Yes, Tuwim took advantage of his superiority, but it was I who seduced him. It entranced him to undress my Plains ignorance. In return, I took his bristles, his eyebrows on my legs, his Jewish guilts.

Early in 1965 he said he had been invited to an East-West conference near a town called L—. I looked it up in an old atlas, where it appeared on the fringes of the Austro-Hungarian empire.

I had published (with his help) my first volume of stories. He said he could get me invited, and I was: with my long legs, my steady mind, my shyness, my red hair, my glasses.

We arrived and were lodged in a villa belonging to the Writers Union. Igor, the congress secretary, who had met Tuwim in Berlin, had invited only personal friends to that villa. They included the Pole (Tadeusz) who gave that first story of mine its ironical name: Luck, the town of.

Throughout the congress, I thought of Igor as overexcited. It seemed a sexual inflammation. Like girls' first love, when all is given. We had plum preserves for breakfast, bread from a wood oven (another of Igor's fellow prisoners was a baker), feather-stuffed duvets. His eyes glistening behind his tinted glasses, lewd, slightly drunk, he seemed in love with the world and its possibilities.

One afternoon, the English girl was stung by a wasp in the depths of the garden. He upended her on a garden bench before she knew what was happening, her hands clutching the hem of her yellow dress; he squeezed, bit, and put his lips (and brilliant teeth) to the soft sole of her foot. And sucked. She flushed and, when he was done, kissed the sting he held on the tip of his tongue.

Another afternoon, he arranged for Tuwim to have his shots. The woman doctor he brought had hands like twigs at the extreme ends of a branch. She couldn't find Tuwim's vein, buried deep and jumping with anxiety. She said, "I haven't had much practice with human veins." Tuwim, stabbed a fourth time, leapt up. He wasn't going to expose his exquisite pattern of blood and circulation to one who ministered to horses (this was in rasping German and that was what he read into the size of her syringe).

A Tuwim tantrum began. Igor ran up the stairs, poked his head through the door, talked to the doctor, and translated. She had meant, "I haven't had much practice with *foreign* veins." She was awed by so many foreign artists. In her eyes, Tuwim could have been Shakespeare.

I went to the marriage of the English girl and the not-so-young Italian, who had pale blue eyes, straight brown hair, charm, and an odd coldness, shyness. When it was over and we all parted, I told Tuwim (who had stayed behind writing his column) that I didn't think much of marriage to start with. In our bed (we had the grandest bedroom, Biedermeier, unreconstructed, unmodernized), Tuwim muttered angrily about unheroics. He was already jealous.

For a Plains woman like me, Igor's was a dazzling, eager seduction. I was taken by the hand and Igor and I jumped the stairs like a gale. Afterward, I lay there and heard provincial weddings in my mind. There was a bandstand by the lake, and one could hear *Nachtmusik* through the thick foliage. I told him what was going on in my head, what dress I was wearing, what flowers I was carrying. Igor asked for the first dance. "When you arrived," he said, "I couldn't imagine you living with that hedgehog."

Dusk took over; we stayed there. Tuwim wasn't on my mind. He wasn't lodged anywhere. But somewhere in the distance, he barked warningly.

Igor was that way with everyone. We were all folded, kneaded, yeasted, warmed. At least in our villa. Only the Russians were excluded. Around *them*, Igor was a beaten dog who whimpers, hunches down, tail tucked between his legs. The night of the ball in the Grand Hotel, the Russians were lined up against a wall: sitting, like Donskoi, on gilt tsarist chairs, or standing, like Breitbourd, gold teeth flashing (who broke his mouth for him once?), his eyes weaving insidiously through the couples on the floor. Igor would not go near them.

In all that time I don't think he had any fear for Matej. If Igor was *ponent*, Matej was *levant*. His fall, his son's rise. In retrospect, what is there to say about Igor and his son? No one looked at Matej too closely; or caught him in his flight. He was transparent, and Igor shone through him. They bore a striking physical resemblance, Matej a taller, leaner version of his father. He was a masculine version of Emöke, a dancer, breastless, lithe.

His room: an eyrie, chaste, sexless except for a bright red coverlet on the narrow bed where Igor and I wrestled. Yes, I think Matej knew we were there. It seemed he was willing his father into love.

•

Since then, I have met the devil in the flesh and I think I begin to understand what happened. A devil wearing black. Tuwim saw him too, but neither of us paid him real attention. We knew nothing about Levitan or the "Night Club" or Emöke. Levitan was just an odd figure who turned up at the round table discussions, which were strictly private. He would pick a chair, look about the room diffidently; then one of the organizers would say, with the utmost courtesy, "this meeting is by invitation only." Levitan would say, "Heaven I see is not for ordinary members of P.E.N.," then leave, with a nasty semiclerical bow.

He tried it several times and caused some small stir. When we could, we skirted him. Still, the congress had taken over this tiny town on the lake, its Grand Hotel, its castle. We invitees crisscrossed along the gravel paths of a spa; we hailed each other across a landscape of bright dots reminiscent of *La Grande Jatte*. And amongst us he loitered, very tall, with a sleek drooping moustache and, usually, a woman on his arm. Once he boated by bearing an umbrella to conceal his recumbent subject. He was Mesmer. The woman clinging to his long fingers or arm was a form to be filled. You could see his purpose. He ate people with his eyes. There were mirrors and dim music in the background, animal magnetism. I had never seen such naked appetite. And not just sexual (undressing), but mental (defrocking). Men, women; on the left, on the right; young, old. Well, they say the devil never wears out his cock.

The Igor in my story was wrong about the boys. At the end of the conference they were all there. I met Viktor's son George personally. He was less frank than Matej. He taught me a new local form of solitaire which he said could also be used to tell fortunes. They were charming youths, very willing. Boyan cycled down to get the L— papers, which gave the full text of Donskoi's speech (that Breitbourd had not translated in its entirety). I also saw them, at the foot of the lawn, in a circle with Levitan.

Levitan was from somewhere near Igor's seaside house. A sort of political Dalmatian Dracula. I don't want to exaggerate the monk-like, the beardless Rasputin, about him. He was secular in bed. With long limbs and boundless, foul energy. Igor says that on his mouth you could see the traces of the hundreds of lips that had crushed themselves against his.

I don't know if that was when Levitan stretched out his long fingers to reach Matej. Does one do to the son as to the father?

What I do know is Matej's room at the villa. I know the tree by the window whose big branch scraped against the gable. When his son wasn't there, Igor used that room to make love. I know I wasn't the only one he made love to. In the same house, we had white magic and black, Igor and Levitan, the dancers and the danced.

This is what happened during the war (Igor told me) to bind them together: A bulb has burned out. In pajamas of parachute silk, Igor stands on a teetering table. Levitan whips Igor's pants down about his knees and in the same gesture puts Igor's cock in his mouth. Igor doesn't move.

Levitan's full history, as recounted by Igor, has already been published: an erotic, cruel history beginning (as far as Igor is concerned) in 1942 with a pimp (Levitan), and two death penalties (Levitan and girl with her head shaven after a madcap honeymoon with an Italian officer in Rome). The sentence was carried out by sending both to Igor's clandestine radio station in the town of L—, which the Germans had discovered and were bombarding daily. Awaiting death, the three of them tell stories. Not New York stories but real histories: such as belong to places like the town of L—. These are some of them:

As a student before the war, brilliant, demoniac, Levitan kills his best friend. He takes pleasure in observing death. His mother (she reappears later) saves him from prison. Papa is dead. Or unknown, which is the same thing. He escapes jail with the help of mitred bishops. But the town of L— pursues him like a pack of dogs. Levitan flees; he signs on board ship; he rigs himself as Rimbaud and sets sail for his *pays de sauvages*.

A boxer, muscular, in Tangier in 1936 he kills a black man.

In Paris in 1937, he cuts the throat of a lodger in the house where he is living: "He got on my nerves," he tells Igor.

He returns home to the town of L—. He takes up with the extreme right. He writes novels which remain unpublished. The war intervenes. Don Giovanni and *Grand Guignol*. Photographers call this sort of recorded life "grainy." For the likes of Levitan, men between eighteen and forty, the choices are not great: God and King (cavalry, swords, etc.); the Germans (women, protection, but who knows the outcome?); the partisans (shoot your enemies, Germans, cavalry, swords, etc.); or hide.

A dancer introduces Igor to Levitan. Igor describes him as a personal *daimon*. What are we to make of such a personage? Have the gods cheated us? May devils too take mud and dust and fashion golems? There are big questions to confront in the nature of creation.

Rich, cultivated, perfumed, a girl comes to work at the station. She is Donna Anna. Levitan comes into Igor's office to announce that that very night he will have her. At three in the morning he wakes Igor, brandishing his fingers under Igor's nose. Fingers that smell of effluvia. He lies beside Igor, who loathes and loves him. The next day, the Germans flee north and they must, now a trio, flee before them. They find a village, an abandoned priest's house. Frozen. Only one blanket per bed, but Levitan has the girl's warm body. A week, ten days go by. One night, Levitan wakes Igor. He holds a finger to his lips and takes him to the churchyard: the girl is laid out in the moonlight with a single shot through her temple. It barely affects her beauty. The skin is punctured only at the point of entry. "They'll never believe it wasn't me," says Levitan. "Give me your gun, I'll shoot myself . . . "

Igor wrestles the gun from him. "Shut up, Levitan. I'll hide the girl for you. No one will know." A carpenter works in the night. In the morning, they bury the girl.

Liberation. Igor takes Levitan to his mother's house. She crosses herself. "He's back," she says. "God save us."

I don't know if any of this is true. A real Levitan exists. But was he as Igor says? Tuwim's doubts, expressed in long, angry letters while I am living with Igor, assail me.

There is a princess, too, later. They are accompanying her back to the town of L—. They stop, Igor, who has become her lover (after rescuing her from disbanding communists), Levitan, and the princess, at an inn. Up late, drinking, inflamed by the princess's perfume, her seductive loftiness, the essence of *avant-guerre*, the two men dispute her favors. Levitan makes obscene suggestions: the princess should be shared. But it is Igor who takes her to bed. The wind howls outside. Below, sounds of an argument, still going on. Igor can hear the innkeeper's and Levitan's voices. Then silence. Igor leaves the princess's opulent body. The innkeeper says, "He's gone, your mad friend." The front door of the inn is wide open to a wilderness of snow.

In the morning, Igor and the princess look for his tracks; drifts cover the mountainside; they return to the inn and prepare to depart. At that point Levitan reappears, his clothes in rags. He throws a bundle of bloody meat on the fresh snow: now they can all eat. They do so and the princess, silent, disappears upstairs with Levitan. When they reach the town of L—, Levitan says, "From now on, I will look after her."

Even as I write, I am terrified by Levitan; by his power over others, which is absolute. Such power is built on scorn for others: not unknowing but intimate. *Sub-iugum*, to put under the yoke, to metamorphose into oxen: one would wake from a man like that drenched in night sweats. He attracted countless victims; was insatiable. There are victims born. No successor-world to Levitan's existed. He cut his swath joyfully in the present.

The trail to Skvorecky's story, *Emöke*, has to do with the fleeting nature of that Luft-town, L—. Emöke herself appears as a spirit hoping to be liberated: in the most unlikely place—a camp for happy socialist workers. She is so delicately here today, gone tomorrow. There is nothing important about love; therefore, nothing important about the loss of love.

"Didn't it ever occur to you to kill him?" I once asked Igor. "There are dangerous animals. When they grow rabid, they are put down."

"You don't understand," he answered. "I don't think he can be killed."

"He killed others. Where's the impunity from?" I was ignorant then of life in L— and angry. At first Levitan seemed to me a sign of weakness in Igor. "You punish people only for political crimes?" I grew heated. (I now reflect that I was jealous of the English girl's sting on his tongue.) "Why don't you strangle him with your bare hands?"

"I wouldn't know for what crime. Anyway, I've forgiven him so many."

"Forgiven?"

He had, in fact, buried the crimes. Buried Donna Anna in a country carpenter's casket. I see him carrying the front end of the coffin into the churchyard, Levitan—much taller, stronger—lurching at the back.

"He owned me. It would have been like killing myself."

"That's admitting that you're dead."

"No. We are merged." Then he gave one of his giggles. "We are one fabulous creature, half him, half me."

The thought of him in Levitan's arms sickened me: a beast with one back. Levitan's long, sinewy arms holding Igor's chest.

It is late at night. Tuwim is off lobbying for his candidate for P.E.N.'s new president and the rest of us have feasted on rabbits. Much wine has been drunk. Only the Italian has been abstemious and watches us from behind his glasses, as from a duck-blind. Matej, his own eyes shining, legs crossed, an elbow on a knee, leaning forward, listens intently. Igor is in the background, extravagant and theatrical, priming himself for his (our) visit to Donskoi at the Marshall's villa. I am in love with both father and son, without understanding either. Not Kansas, not graduate school, not eighteen months in New York, have prepared me for *this* Europe, for the debris of totalitarianism, for prisons, psychopaths, and living aslant the world.

Later I asked Tuwim—impatient as ever when I wanted to talk about Igor (about whom he had already begun writing)—"Why do you think this Levitan chose Igor? Was it some failing in him? Or something too desirable?"

Tuwim tolerated no third sex. Natural functions were gross, but they had a purpose. Remove any possible end from the act and you had the unnatural: sex for the mechanical pleasure. He said, "Because the man's a woman."

My Igor? Years in an emotional brothel, learning all the tricks, yes. For someone plain like myself, a delicious lover, full of flutterings and flatteries. Homosexuality did not enter into it. What had happened to him with Levitan was subjection, not something in himself. He did not deny having belonged to Levitan (belonging to him still?), but the nature of that belonging was not affective. He had been seized. I now felt I had betrayed Igor by telling Tuwim about Levitan. It was then I decided Tuwim had more in common with Levitan than I had realized. He felt with his mind.

I had to make my farewells to Igor during the fireworks at the congress's close. I knew the young men were all there, among the crenellations, between steep, pitched roofs. Tuwim had planned an early departure to catch the express to Venice: one night there and we would go back to New York via Milan. Departure was a child I might be bearing, I felt so heavy. Igor looked out from the parapets (I could see Matej out of the corner of my eye, a shadow lit by intermittent star bursts) and said, "We don't really exist, do we?"

I said I might come back. But I wouldn't be real here, would I? No more than I could see Igor in New York. He knew there would be repercussions. He took his glasses off and sat down with his back to the wall. "I want to go to sleep," he said.

The next morning Matej drove us to the station in the town of L—. It was the first time he had driven alone. He carried our bags in. He kissed me on the cheek. He said, "Don't come back unless you want to. The best ones leave."

Uncomfortably strapped into our seats across the Atlantic, Tuwim and I argued (nor had Venice been a happy night). After his third martini, already in New York in his head, he said crossly: "You just don't know anything, do you? Igor wasn't in jail for political reasons. I asked around. He was in there because he was a fag, a disgrace. He was accused of pederasty, this Levitan was a witness. This is one of those places where buggery isn't chic."

We ate from our plastic trays in silence. "It is just like you to fall in love with an Igor," he said during the darkened hours of the film. "With that Europe and its Turkish plots. How could he survive if he wasn't a communist? Isn't he Secretary to the Academy? Maybe they didn't really love Stalin, but he was their mamma. They kowtowed and obeyed so they wouldn't lose his love."

I lost my patience; I wanted to put a fist through Alitalia's padded fuselage and blow us all up. "What a moral prick you are!" I said. "You grew up at the *Partisan Review*. You went weak at the knees too. You suckled at the same tit."

"I was weaned early," Tuwim answered.

"Not early enough."

Tuwim was happy with an argument. The trouble with him was, he was not just insistent, he was unremitting. Phlegm, bile, blood, choler, he had all the humors. "Okay, I regret that period in my life. But no one compelled those people in eastern Europe. They *knew* what the system was like. They weren't just your Sartre and Bertie Russell, Chomsky and Neruda, living out a fantasy. Your Igor's as gutless as the rest of them."

I'm a nonpolitical person. I believe all things are ultimately personal. I see the body politic as just another body: a greedy nose, its snout in the trough, ears that eavesdrop on private conversations, all-seeing eyes and blind eyes as well. The body marches on heavy feet, slaps you on the back with a hearty hand. Its brain is invisible, controlling the visible. Its intestines are history.

When Igor wrote that he was in trouble with the authorities, I thought to get away for a few weeks. Igor didn't ask me to come and, remembering his son's advice (how could I say I *wanted* to go back?), when I did make up my mind, I thought I was doing no more than laying a wreath on last summer's fling.

I arrived in the town of L— to find that Igor had been summoned back to the castle on the lake. A small committee of the Writers Union was assembled there to go through accounts, to render its report, to write to David in London and reassure him that all was well—though nothing had happened since and the world of culture and letters had gone safely back to sleep in the town of L—.

I was met at the airport by Matej, notably pale, formal. In the months since the meeting, it seemed as if he'd grown up: too fast, without ballast. It was an ugly, squally day; he had mastered the car (which was Marek's) and it no longer gave him pleasure. In Igor's tiny basement, I felt the oppression of all those cupboards and wooden recesses, the furniture that slotted back into the walls. These two prison friends (Marek and Igor) had recreated their cell, as shut away from the rest of the town as their Europe was insulated from the world.

It was all about the fireworks, Igor said. Here there was always an aftermath, petty revenge. He faced the committee, from a high-backed chair in what had been the throne room. Igor was shame-faced, they were cautious, smooth, and well dressed. They had all the right words, the correct formulations. Igor was distracted and played the *boulevardier*. Perhaps the most pitilessly correct of them all was Viktor.

What could I do, sitting on a remote chair against a chill wall? I who was (perhaps) part of what they called the "scandal." "Don't worry," Igor said, "they can't really touch me. Josip is on my side." And yes, they were frightened of the President of the Academy, but they could nibble at the old man's edges through someone like Igor whom he plainly loved. Igor might have protection: all the more reason for them to protect themselves against him. Pettiness grew like a camel hump on their backs.

Did he think they weren't aware of the play he was planning ("Not even your cast agrees with you"); that they couldn't discern his true intent? Or of the stories he told during the meetings, malign stories, gratuitous insults? Of how he treated the Union's villa as a private playground among foreigners who didn't understand the ways of the country? ("A man in your position should learn to keep his private life to himself.") Furthermore, Viktor said severely, they had a report from Professor Levitan about Matej and his companions. "We cannot have your son occupying a room in a villa belonging to the Writers Union where you conduct your scandalous affairs. How do we know what meetings he held there with other boys? We have to think about our own children, and his influence on them."

I saw Igor stand up, holding onto the back of his tall chair. He said,

"Matej has always gone there when he liked. It's his second home."

"They all have too much freedom."

"No more argument," another member of the Committee said. "The President has agreed. We have voted."

Poor Josip. The old man had been forced to yield to keep Igor safe. I thought about the three sisters, so ambiguously decorous, so cavalier. And about that little room on the top floor of the villa. I had the feeling that, out of defiance if for no other reason, Matej and the others, perhaps even the three sisters, when they went missing from the town of L—, went there. It had the feeling of a room in which plots were hatched. As the Union Committee droned on—now they were considering the fireworks ("A scandalous unauthorized expenditure which you cannot expect the Union to pay.")—through peculiar tears of my own, I saw the red bed in that room.

Suddenly, Igor came to me in the back of the great high-walled room. Dead white, his eyes hidden by his blue glasses, he took me by the hand as though for another of our urgent seductions. Only he was shaking, his shoulders hunched up against his ears, his arms clutching his ribs as though in a freezing wind.

"Our children," he said. Was he mocking Viktor's words?

Together we climbed the sharply-curving stone steps to the tower, and from the top he looked out over the lake, anxious but— it being dark—unable to see. Not the boat in which we had rowed out to the island, not the island, not the church tower. In short, nothing that was to happen.

What *did* happen I heard from a distance, after I had gone back to New York, and just as I was beginning *The Town of Luck*, a story which was meant to be quite different.

In New York, Tuwim's scrutiny was constant and I resolved to free myself from the weight of his bile. Daily he sat on the Upper West Side writing his book. Proofreading it for him, I saw Igor being squeezed out, into the margins. In my own study, I wrote about the horror of Levitan with his arms around Igor. In the same way, Tuwim had his moral arms, an iron maiden, around Igor.

I heard, in my imagination first, and then by means of a brief, heartrending letter from Igor, the gravel creak with heavy boots as his son was borne away and down, from air to earth. "How can I even ask you?" he wrote pitiably, immersed in memories of the lake in which love was never mentioned, in which a simple human need was uppermost. "I have nothing to give you. I can only take."

I rewrote my story, adding Matej's death and those of the other bright young men of L—. But the story did not, could not, explain how the son, an Ariel, a creature of light, could have died; and how the father could have survived.

Amongst other things, Igor's letter made it plain there was nothing I could do. There were losses in the town of L—. They had to do with the way they lived there, with what they were, with their history, their histories. He said there was no living with the ghost of his son, with his posters on the wall (atomic structures, Descartes, a bare alp) or his jeans on the hook.

Tuwim wasn't without sympathy. "All the parents must have been devastated," he said. "He," meaning Matej, "was such a beautiful boy."

I think that in the little time I stayed in New York after Matej's death, my mind in the town of L—, Igor remained in Tuwim's mind, though we made it a rule, as our relationship drew to a close, not to speak of him. I came to realize that I had never felt closer to love, which Igor had given to me with as much abandon as he gave it to his son, than in L—. That was where I belonged.

III

The state of the play is this: I went back again to the town of L—. Why? Igor didn't ask me to. There had seemed to be, when I left (the second time, after the Writers Union meeting), nothing to say. When I said I was going back, Tuwim was bitter. He thought I was using Igor as a pretext to leave him.

"You feel sorry for the poor bugger. How midwestern of you! The son kills himself on some whim; the father, you say, has been bullied by the state; the brightest kids play Dostoyevsky while their fathers read Marx and buy perfume in Paris. What's that alongside the slaughter of Jews or the Gulag?" He thought I yearned for victim status myself. "You want to know why suffering is so irrelevant to Americans that they can worry about smoking and the fruit fly. You feel you ought to be involved in greater disasters."

I heard it all in Igor's letters. Levitan was found burned in the Mercedes of a German tourist. It was said in L— that the German had served there during the war.

Igor wrote: "Matej's body was still warm. Levitan hanged him. He carried him in his arms and hanged him."

I arrived in a belted raincoat in midwinter, carrying little: perhaps some idea of healing. We settled, Igor and I, by the sea, where we were happy for many years.

On arrival, I found this complex man, the Igor I loved, in convalescence from repudiation—that is, the town again crossed the street to avoid him. What we lived through together, in the early years, was not so much *skandal* as the Evil Eye. People like Viktor withdrew into privacy. Collectively, the town's fathers fled somewhere inside themselves. Josip died. The three sisters were packed away, together with the salon, into widowhood. Olga had married; Xenija had an affair with a Parisian dancer and played a bit part in a Fellini film. These were signs of the times.

But the deaths of four youths (another had followed Matej) clung to Igor for some years. There were still three other families in mourning. There were conjectures, explanations, even a cheap book (as Igor was writing his own), asking why the police had carried off the young men and buried them so expeditiously, made no inquiries, never questioned Levitan. A magazine offered a Marxist interpretation (the discontents of the bourgeoisie).

No one wrote from the abroad of which so much had been made at the round tables. Don Pablo was silent; the English poets played games. The one exception was a Paraguayan who sent Igor his verses, inscribed.

Back home in L— for the winter, the dogs bayed. With my dollars we worked our way out of one desolation. We flung our firework money at the Union's feet; they nodded implacably. Their eyes asked, what was I doing there? *Spijonaźa?* Prison theater was out, the actors disbanded. We went to Boyan's grave and dropped pink flowers on the snow and laughter formed around Igor like condensation—he was remembering Boyan as Ophelia.

At the first signs of spring, we rowed out to the island on the lake. Marek was with us and he gave me a few more details while

Igor was up in the church tower (I note how often high places figure in this story): how he had not gone away as Igor told him to, but followed him in the snow, first up to the villa, then down to the boathouse, then watched him glide across the lake. "He knew," Marek said.

"Did Levitan kill him? If so, where was he? Hiding on the island? Did he row out with Matej?"

"Levitan is dead."

I asked him how such a wound could heal if there was no explanation. Gnarled, a body cut of wood, Marek shrugged. Why should there be an explanation? I said (because I was then, I already knew, bearing Igor's son): "Because it has to do with his father, doesn't it?"

"If I were you, *Gospá*, I would not ask." He was sullen, stolid, silent. Igor rang the bell in the tower.

I felt a wave of sadness: no matter how many sons I bore Igor, I could not replace Matej. This new me was angry; I was defending my own son. I said: "If Levitan killed him, where was he? You were there. Did you see him?" My voice rose: "You were there, couldn't you have saved him?"

A wet wind was blowing down from the mountains. Buds had barely formed on the trees. Marek spat on the ground. He crossed himself when the bell rang (or when I mentioned Levitan). But I couldn't force my way through his reluctance. I couldn't touch a loyalty built in prison, where Levitan had also been. That was the beginning and end of a tangled skein: the war, subjugation, prison.

Now, twenty years later, I recognize that there is a human dimension to this story that I hadn't perceived. It has to do with the nature of the town of L—. And it is that if one constructs a metaphor for one's life, one must live in it. Matej had his Emöke, Igor his firehouse, his high-wire, his *daimon*. I represented Kansas, endless, boundless, flat. The snow on L—'s streets, the winter wind, were as sharp as those of my childhood, but I notice that even in the way I write about those snows, and mark them as a passing of time (the years went by, I now had two boys), they have another dimension. When I sometimes try to explain my childhood to Yuri and Daniel, no voice enters the warm kitchen from a radio propped over the stove and tells the citizens of L— the windchill factor or that school will be closed today. Bells ring, fireworks go off: everything has meaning. But there is no common sense. These are people of a more acrobatic stage, more accustomed to metaphor than to the real world. One is to take them at that metaphorical level, for no other will do.

In this way, Tuwim was right. I became infected by it myself. I too made gestures. I *chose* the town of L—. The ill-lit streets that wound up to the upper town (I now carried a string bag hanging from my arm and we brought chickens back from the coast together) immured me. Neon was far away.

I have said we were happy, and we were. Each of us had two lives, and we were happy in the one we had together. My other life was made of questioning. I can give no explanation, I only know that at some point in life one wants to draw on truth. Little else will do. All the big questions ultimately require answering. For all I had shed by then (my wardrobe, my glasses, the redness of my hair, the lankness of my body), the questions remained and the truth had to be ascertained.

Igor's other life was made of what had been before I was. Sometimes, he could make this bitterly plain: if, while holding Yuri and Daniel, I mentioned their dead brother, he would say, "I cannot forget Matej, but I want to do the thinking about him, and no one else should."

Ultimately, I could not live with the ambiguity in Igor. Not knowing which man he was, which story was true, which town, which death, was real, which wasn't. I could not live in the town of L—. Nor could I live with Igor's memories, or with the memory of him. And eventually I took our two children back to New York. There, in Tuwim's words, we lived as exiles. The children are emigrés. And the ghost of the older brother is present (as is that of the father).

Tuwim had grown old, and the hair that used to bristle in his eyebrows now sprouted from his ears. As his students abandoned him for newer gods, he became bitter and angry.

I have abandonments to make myself. I will cease to write stories. I have begun to earn a living at a glossy magazine where I edit other people's imaginings and no longer dwell on my own. Tuwim's book is about to appear, so many years later. He has not changed his opinions of any of the men he writes about; he has merely enlarged them to constitute a scenario of defeat, shame, blame. That other Europe, he says, is a place where nothing happens. Even its revolutions are only apparent. There is neglect and waste in history, and human lives are not worth mentioning in the same breath as quarrels of the mind. This is a low-overhead view; it requires no investment.

Carrying an image of a man I loved and with whom I was happy, and of his firstborn, resplendent then, with everything before him that I thought I had before me, and also certain darker images, my Igor undone, I renounce fictions.

Yes. A wind blew through the town of L—, too: to finish my story, to put *kônec*, the end (as I saw on so many screens while there), to some of its history, too.

About two years ago now, the wind began to blow. The town of L— had its own oblique demonstrations. Oblique, as was their way there. Oblique as the demonstrations of four young men twenty years before. There were actors. The streets were theater and the theater was opened again. Young people with painted lips and garish colors on cheeks of fine chalk massed and sang and painted liberating slogans on walls.

Igor, who had been "rehabilitated," had a new play on. His actors all wore giant ears, larger than elephants' ears, which stuck out from the sides of their heads. Igor, too, wore ears. A *chapeau melon*, like the rest, perched between his huge ears, baggy pants, a little black moustache, a twirling stick. They jigged and twirled through the curving streets from the old town downwards. By then, people no longer crossed to the other side of the street. A huge amount was now forgotten. Instead, there were children following them (it was summer and they wore shorts and cotton shirts) and barking dogs which no longer threatened.

In front, walking an imaginary wire, laughing, sleeping, Igor shows how an acrobat falls, how he plucks out his heart and tosses it lightheartedly to the public assembled below. At that moment, on the curb, he rights himself, gesticulates with his stick, falls backward and is struck (perhaps obliquely, metaphorically) by a police car.

In another version, the dogs catch up and drive him from the sidewalk; he defends himself by tilting at them, as at windmills; their snarls grow fiercer and he flees into the oncoming car.

It was a stupid death and I was informed of it by a voice without sorrow as I sat by the sea with my two sons, his two sons.

I have in front of me the first sentence I wrote about Igor, when I was imagining him and simply concerned, as a writer, with portraying to myself a man I knew very well and didn't know. I was writing in anger, I'm sorry to say (it was when I came back to America for the second time), and what I wrote was: "Igor had much charm, led a charmed life but, unlike his son, died a quick, stupid death."

In the son's lay the father's.

Now events have overtaken that sentence. Igor is now the dots on a news photo. He is in Tuwim's book, who concludes that a sadness overcomes him to think that some histories may be forgotten.

That may be, and need not be, a reason for writing this one.

Author's note: A town called Luck exists, only it is called Łuck (Wutsk) and isn't the real town where this story took place: but who could resist such a name? The rest of the story is more true, and it is borrowed from Joze Javoršek, the Slovene writer who figures here as Igor. There was a suicide club, and Joze had a son who took his own life. There also was a Levitan. I translated Joze's story and it was published the week he died. Emöke comes from a story by Jozef Skvorećky. —K.B.

Pericles, Prince of Tyre:
A Commentary

For Michael Dobson, onlie instigator

I

What makes a man? Ruby, carbuncle, beryl
and sard, all the purple dye in Tyre;
jasper, sunstone, chalcedony, the blood
-red carnelian. What makes a man the answer

to a riddle locked in a jeweled box? Find him
at home in storms (*he puts on sackcloth
and to sea*), backdrop of stitched cloudbanks
and paste gems cast into a cardboard surge

while Gower plays a red guitar.

What man marries a casket drowned at sea
and dedicates it to Diana? *Convey thy Deity
aboard our dancing boat.* Behold our hero, Pericles.
The moon exerts its pull on his unshaven hair,

his wave-lost head: steers him to Tarsus
and Pentapolis, Mytilene and Ephesus, a wayward tide
lashing the coast of Asia Minor. Great is Diana
descending from the ceiling in a gilded cage

when Gower plays his red guitar.

Someone has come to rob Marina of her maiden's jewel
and make himself a man of means. Another man
comes by her at a gallant price, and buys himself
a crown of gold, studded with garnet cabochons

and the signet of a full-blown sail, the canvas swell
mastered by song. She is a woman not of any shores,
where she was never born. *Thou art a man, and I*
have suffered like a girl. The gods make her prosperous

though Gower plays a red guitar.

Some men marry their daughters rather than barter them
for sons, and some are sung from marine despair
by children's voices that they recognize
as home, *where all the waters meet.* The ballad

bears his burden, pours a corroded pail of gales
over his unwashed head to rust a trawler's net
of chain-mail armor in an undertow. The iron
found in the hand makes him a man

when Gower plays his red guitar.

II

Behold our hero, Pericles, once a man
of parts, and now a man apart
from banks and harbors, from anywhere
but wind-lashed waves and thunderheads. His plot
is wandering, the answer to his riddle

nowhere on earth. The hero is identified
by all the places left behind (*What seas, what shores*
what gray rocks and what islands), his commerce
with the open sea, trading a wife
for an auspicious gale, a daughter for

safe landfall. Landless, a daughter trades
her talents for virginity, her qualities
for a customer become a husband
by a found father's will. Of her ledgers
of these transactions not a trace

remains, erased in recognition's tide
of tears: a current that will take her
back to a Tyre she's never seen, built on trade
in textiles, cinnabar, and wheat. So she has lost
a mother twice, and gained a governor for father

of her father's heirs, another woman traded
between two men of means to make the marriage plot.
*And woodthrush calling through the fog, My
daughter.* You'll wear purple, girl, and cloth-of-gold,
and spin your tale in tapestries no one will read.

*Bring me spices, ink and paper, My casket
and my jewels. Bring me the satin coffin.*

III

Thaisa loves a man of no renown, and with a name
to come. That's Homer, by way of Pound, and somewhat
misremembered. Like the play, like Pericles,

who misremembers who he is and has to be reminded
by a mislaid child, whom he has missed
without quite having met. (She is a woman

made of stone, a statue overlooking Tarsus
harbor, thighs sealed shut as a tomb, cold
to Lysimachus's advance. There is no private place, none

where they are not watched.) A text abducted
like a daughter pirates seize, the play predicts
its fragments, is predicated on them. A romance

that rounds upon itself (rousing but a bit
ridiculous, and recognizing itself so), this *song
that old was sung* revises its own tune. We may ascribe

the plot's lacunae to a nodding scribe, or to an actor's lapse
in memory, judgment. *Th'unfriendly elements*
forget thee utterly. We reconstruct the juncture

out of conjecture, and take our parts in the play:
the lines corrupt, and bracketed by gaps. Bracketed
by transactions in textiles and well-born virgins,

sea-tossed, Pericles thwarts one role after another, *driven*
before the winds over a painted backcloth wave,
scraps of wayward canvas sewn into a rotting sail. He's a prince

among men, this man she's set her course
on marrying before she knows his name: he never tires
of wandering from Tyre, *where we left him,*

on the sea. Knock on the moon and the stars
come out of clouds to guide his barque,
knock on the stars and the door is opened

to a temple in Ephesus where a coffined wife's cabochon
has navigated Neptune's sea of asterisks and breakers,
cast ashore like driftglass smoothed to opal, pearl:

the woman he weeps to lose and find alike.

A Conversation

Collage For Bruce Conner, 1973.
Photo collage and telephone dial on paper, 10 ¾ x 4 ⅛ in.
p. 225

Untitled (study for September Blackberries), c. 1972.
Photo collage, oil, and acrylic on paper, 7 ⁵/₉ x 7 ⅝ in.
p. 226

Untitled (for B.C.), 1973.
Photo collage, 4 ⅞ x 6 ½ in.
p. 227

Untitled, 1973.
Photo collage, 8 ⅜ x 6 ¾ in.
p. 228

Untitled (for B.C.), 1973.
Photo collage, 9 ¾ x 7 ¾ in.
p. 229

Untitled (for B.C.), 1973.
Photo collage, 9 ½ x 7 ⁷/₁₆ in.
p. 230

Untitled (for B.C.), 1973.
Photo collage, 14 ½ x 7 in.
p. 231

Untitled, 1972–73.
Photo collage and tape, 10 ½ x 15 in.
p. 232

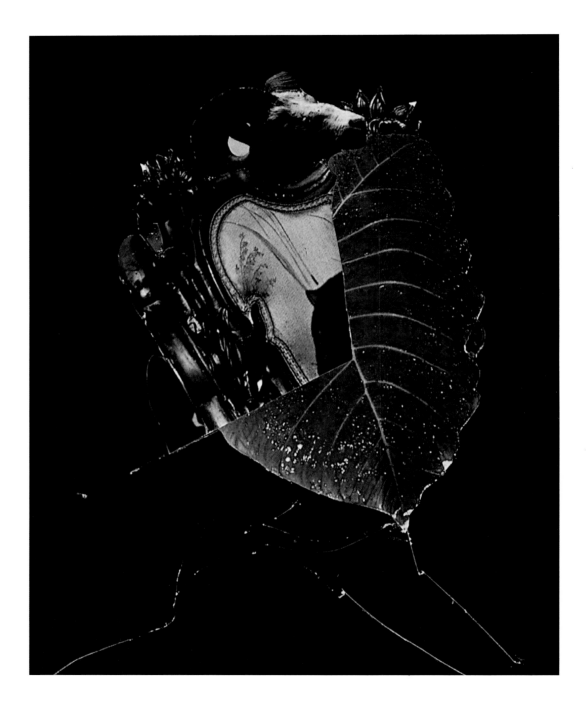

Jay DeFeo's life entered into the working (and reworking) of more than a ton of black and white oil paint on canvas. It was titled *The Death Rose*, later called *The White Rose*, and finally *The Rose* in 1965. It was a masterpiece of spirit and transformation that almost destroyed her through lead poisoning and its dominance over her relationship to the conscious world. When Jay and *The Rose* were evicted by their landlord, the thread was lost and Jay's life unraveled. The painting disappeared behind a wall and has not been seen since the 1970s.

Jay worked on *The Rose* for seven years to the virtual exclusion of any other artwork. It took her another seven years, the amount of time it takes to replace every cell in the human body, before she could begin to reassemble the parts into a whole image. The fragments of value around her in a small house among the redwoods north of San Francisco were photographed and collaged and rephotographed as the most solid images her mind could bring close and secure. She chose the objects that she saved and used from the past as if they were holy artifacts and a part of the true cross: a tripod, teeth, goggles, jewelry of her own design, a golf bag, an old upright telephone with a flame-shaped bulb replacing the receiver. Using acrylic, charcoal, graphite, ink, and wax pencil, she rendered these objects into elegant black-and-white images which imply the structure or parts of the body. They are without proportion and seem to have a vibrance which is tightly held from dissipation.

The photo collages literally acted out the process of assimilation by allowing the images to move about, change their relationships, and transform into a variety of forms. They were important in the process of creating the later paintings and drawings. They began in 1972–1973 as purely personal notes in a visual diary. The images of her drawings and paintings and photographs constantly worked with each other: a collage could direct her vision for a painting, and the painting could then carry on a dialogue with the camera and photo collages. The objects themselves obtained a controlled voice by association: a telephone could transform itself into a golf bag or a human figure or a flower, like a scene in a Betty Boop cartoon.

The collages here that are titled "for Bruce Conner" have reference to the marathon telephone conversations we indulged in between San Francisco and her northern house. Both of us needed to be talked through a perceived crisis of identity within our work. I mailed her the dial from a telephone with my phone number printed in the center. She cut out a figure that refers to the full body photograms I had recently made and attached the dial to the figure as though it were the telephone. I had become the telephone. I asked her to keep the collages instead of accepting them as a gift, and they remained with her from then on. I asked for, and received, the footstool she used when painting *The Rose* for seven years. She attached a note to the footstool. It said:

> *For Bruce*
> *love, Jay*
> *("we are not what*
> *we seem")*

—Bruce Conner

The Game of Truth

Advancing among the aloes and palms along the beach-front, in the rosy light of late afternoon, the old poet, frail in his tan colonial suit, was the image of decline. He looked at the passersby with a blissful smile and closed his eyes.

"That's your hotel, Maestro," said the woman, who was holding him by the arm.

"But it isn't the Majestic?" he asked, stopping and raising his stick at the immense building, with its white balconies, and flags fluttering in the warm breeze.

"No, it's just the Imperial," answered the woman patiently, pushing him gently toward the opposite sidewalk.

They crossed the street and entered the cool half-shadow of the lobby. In the corner to the left a few guests, nearly hidden in velvet armchairs, were watching a tennis match on television.

A young woman with curly hair and a tape recorder slung over her shoulder came toward them smiling: "May I ask you some questions for a local radio program?"

"No, the Maestro is tired," his companion intervened.

"Let her speak," said the poet kindly. "Will it take long?"

"No, though it's not very short," the girl answered, reassured. She looked at him with luminous eyes, ignoring his companion. "It's a special sort of program, different from the usual."

"What is it?"

"It's called the Game of Truth, and you have to say the opposite of what you think."

"Ah," the poet nodded. "But people do that all the time."

"Yes, but without saying so. Here, instead, we announce it at the beginning of the broadcast. You say the opposite of the truth, and we get to know the truth, but in a more entertaining way."

The poet gazed at her with curiosity.

"And, besides, we discover your way of lying," the girl continued. "Do you lie often?"

"Are we already on the air?" asked the poet, looking at the tape recorder.

"Oh no!" The girl smiled. "But let's imagine we are. What would you answer?"

"That I never lie."

"Then you mean that you always lie?"

The poet shook his head. "No, that's not true, either."

"Then it is true?"

The poet smiled, embarrassed. "No, you're confusing me. At my age the reflexes are no longer so quick. But the idea appeals to me."

He turned to his companion, who was listening with silent disapproval.

"Should I go and rest a little?" It was not clear whether he was asking a question or making a statement. "We could meet here in half an hour."

"Terrific!" the girl said.

"All right, then." The poet bowed slightly as he shook her hand. "In a little while."

They chose a corner near a large window, screened by two hedges of evergreens, where the noise from the lobby was muffled, and the people outside passed silently behind the glass.

The poet and the girl sat on a semicircular sofa, while the poet's companion took an armchair opposite and turned it to look out the window.

"All right. Can we begin?" the girl asked, with the tape recorder on her lap. And as the poet nodded she pressed two buttons on the recorder. "Here we are, dear friends, in the lobby of the Hotel Imperial, in the company of the illustrious guest whose biography you have just heard."

From the moment she began to speak, gazing at the microphone, she seemed to be somewhere else, in a euphoric space of her own.

"Our guest, dear friends, has readily agreed to the rules of our game, the Game of Truth. So let's start immediately, with the first question. Are you pleased that tonight our mayor is bestowing honorary citizenship on you?"

"No."

"Very good. And what do you like about our city?"

What did he like? Almost nothing, now. He saw again the pebbly beach just after the war, and the still-empty hotels along the sea. This uninhabited world had attracted him then, he did not know why.

"Almost everything," he answered.

"What! Everything?" the girl exclaimed. "You should have said 'Nothing,' don't you think?"

"Yes, nothing," he murmured. "I got mixed up."

"We understood that." The girl smiled. "It happens to many of the guests on the Game of Truth. The problem with lying is getting used to it. But now let's go on to other questions, and please try to answer immediately. Are you happy with yourself?"

"Yes."

"And with life?"

"Yes."

"Good," the girl said. "I see you're entering into the spirit of the game. Would you like to be a few years younger?"

"No."

"What does it mean, to you, to be mature?"

It was to bow to the facts.

"I don't know," he answered.

"Then you do know. Tell us."

In a little while he would disappear, this was what he knew.

"Perhaps it is a line from a Russian poet whose name I've forgotten, a name with two syllables. But I remember the line, it's a triple prohibition: 'Do not fear, do not hope, do not ask.'"

"But what a pessimist you are! You don't believe that's an exaggeration?"

"No. Or rather, yes. You decide."

"And what were your ambitions like?"

He saw himself as a boy again, coming out of the village library, and in his right hand he was holding a soiled, damaged book of poetry. The world was in that book, and so he carried it delicately.

"Modest," he replied.

"And do you feel fulfilled?"

This too was a word he was not fond of; he no longer recognized himself in what the others were saying.

He rested his hand on the girl's hand. "Don't you want to start again from the beginning? But with an ordinary interview. You ask the usual questions and I'll give you the usual answers. I don't know the truth; yet you imagine I know the opposite."

"All right," the girl said, with regret. She had pressed a button on the tape recorder and put it on the table.

"I understand that you're not good at lying," she added.

"Not true," the poet said. "I would not have survived to this age."

"Well, this is already a definition of lying," the girl nodded. "And about the truth, what can you tell me?"

The poet looked at her. "About the truth I prefer to keep silent," he said.

Sitting in a wicker armchair in front of the open window, the poet saw, parallel to the balustrade, the line of the sea. The wind had stopped and offshore the water was a sparkling stripe. A battleship was motionless in the center of the view. What was that type of ship called? No, not vessel. It was a two-syllable word, but he couldn't remember it. It seemed to him that the word ended in "er," but the first part was blurry—maybe it began with "c," like crew. He felt that he was getting close, but he must not insist, perhaps he should even distance himself, think of something else. Once, on television, a brain specialist had talked about senile marasmus: that was a term he had never forgotten, senile marasmus, even though, if he thought about it, it did not fit his case. "Marasmus" made him think of disorder, chaos. In his case it was, rather, as if the brain were silently caving in and he had run to safety, far away. Then, turning, he saw only ruins and the dust rising from crumbling pavilions. Powerless, resigned, he watched his own dissolution, which reminded him of a tall building (three syllables) he had seen on television, shot in slow motion as it collapsed on itself. Perhaps it had introduced a program about disasters. The sequence was then shown in reverse, and the building returned in a moment to what it had been before.

He rose slowly from the chair and leaned on the balustrade. In the street below pedestrians were swarming among the cars. Black rocks protected the road from the waves, but occasionally the spray reached the sidewalk.

A flock of birds rose from the pier. He saw their name—two syllables—circle above the water of the harbor, then turn toward the coast and come to roost on the rocks. No, he could not have forgotten that, he had even named them once in a poem. He half closed his eyes. The air was cool, salty. "Seagulls," he murmured.

Translated from the Italian by Ann Goldstein

Olie Anderson runs Olie Anderson's 4X4 Daredevils, a traveling stunt and daredevil performance show. He has worked in the daredevil profession for over thirty years and is one of the few performers alive today who has jumped a car over 160 feet through the air. He is based in Neola, Utah.

Anthea Bell lives in Cambridge, England.

Walter Benjamin, a seminal German critic and cultural theorist, was born in Berlin in 1892. *Berlin Childhood in Nineteen Hundred* was first published in 1950, a decade after Benjamin died during an attempt to cross the Pyrenees from occupied France into Spain.

Keith Botsford's stories and articles have appeared in magazines and newspapers, including *The Paris Review, The Independent* (London), and journals in France, Hungary, Israel, and the Czech Republic. He is a former editor of *The Noble Savage* and the current editor of *Bostonia*, and has published several novels pseudonymously.

Chris Burden was born in Boston, Massachusetts in 1946. His recent solo exhibitions include those at the Lannan Foundation, Los Angeles, the Whitechapel Art Gallery, London, the Brooklyn Museum, and the Institute of Contemporary Art, Boston. Recent group exhibitions include the 1989 Whitney Biennial, *Helter Skelter* at the Museum of Contemporary Art, Los Angeles, *Dislocations* at the Museum of Modern Art, New York, and *Virtual Reality* at the Australian National Gallery, Canberra. He lives and works in Topanga, California and is represented by the Gagosian Gallery, New York.

Bruce Conner is an artist living and working in San Francisco. He invented electricity in 1957.

Donna De Cesare is a freelance photographer. Her photographs have appeared in publications such as *Aperture, The New York Times Magazine, The Atlantic*, and *Newsweek*. Her work has been exhibited most recently at Artist Space, New York. She is currently working with Luis J. Rodriguez on a book about the transference of Los Angeles gang culture to El Salvador. This work was begun with the support of the Center for Documentary Studies at Duke University.

Georganne Deen was born in Fort Worth, Texas in 1951. She has exhibited throughout the United States, most recently at the Laguna Beach Art Museum and Exit Art, New York. Solo exhibitions of her work have been held at Fred Hoffman Gallery and Zero One in Los Angeles. She lives and works in Los Angeles.

Jay DeFeo was born in Hanover, New Hampshire in 1929. She was a significant figure in the Northern California art world in the 1950s and '60s, a community which included artists Bruce Conner and Wallace Berman. She was also active in Los Angeles, where she was involved with the seminal Ferus Gallery. Her work was included in *Sixteen Americans* at the Museum of Modern Art, New York, in 1959—an exhibition which introduced then-emerging artists Robert Rauschenberg, Louise Nevelson, and Frank Stella, among others. Her long career included exhibitions at the San Francisco Museum of Modern Art, the Oakland Museum, and the University Art Museum, Berkeley. A survey of her drawings and photo collages from the 1970s was recently mounted at Kohn Turner Gallery, Los Angeles. Her work will appear in the upcoming *Beat Culture and The New America 1950–1965* at the Whitney Museum of American Art, New York. She died on November 11, 1989.

Ann Goldstein is working on a translation of Pier Paolo Pasolini's last novel, *Petrolio.*

Dana Hábova lives and works in Prague, where she creates subtitles for English-language films.

Brooks Hansen was born in New York City in 1965. His first novel, *Boone* (Summit), cowritten with Nick Davis, was published in 1990. *The Origami Knight* is adapted from his forthcoming second novel *The Chess Garden*, to be published by Farrar, Straus & Giroux in 1995.

Roald Hoffmann writes poetry and essays, but makes a living as a theoretical chemist. He has published two poetry collections, *The Metamict State* and *Gaps and Verges* (University of Central Florida Press), and a nonfiction volume, *The Same and Not the Same*, will be published by Columbia University Press in April 1995.

CONTRIBUTORS

Miroslav Holub, one of Europe's foremost poets, lives and works in Prague. His most recent collection of poems, published in the U.K. by Faber & Faber and in the U.S. by Oberlin College Press, is *Vanishing Lung Syndrome*.

Dennis Hopper is a film director, photographer, painter, and actor who appeared most recently in *Speed* and *Red Rock West*. He also appears in the forthcoming *Waterworld*. The movies he has directed include *Easy Rider, Colors, The Hot Spot,* and most recently *Chasers*. Exhibitions of his visual work have been held in Barcelona, Paris, Boston, New York, and Los Angeles.

Fanny Howe's most recent novel is *Saving History* (Sun & Moon Books), her most recent collection of poetry, *The End* (Littoral Books).

Matt Jasper washes dishes in a restaurant owned by his wife and ex-wife in Dover, New Hampshire. He is a frequent contributor to *Foot Worship News, Roller Derby,* and *The Flat Earth Society* newsletter.

Michael Klonovsky is a journalist. He lives in Munich, Germany.

Annie Leibovitz began taking photographs for *Rolling Stone* while still a student at the San Francisco Art Institute. She became the magazine's chief photographer in 1973 at the age of 22. Her work has since appeared in *LIFE, Time, Newsweek, Vogue, Esquire,* and *Vanity Fair*. A collection of her work, *Photographs: Annie Leibovitz, 1970–1990,* was published by Harper-Collins in 1992.

Deborah Levy is a poet, playwright, novelist, and performance artist. Her novels include *Ophelia and the Great Idea, Beautiful Mutants, Swallowing Geography,* and *The Unloved,* and her journalism has appeared in *Vogue, The New Statesman, The Guardian,* and *The Independent*. She lives and works in London.

David Mamet is the author of various plays, including *American Buffalo, Speed-the-Plow, Glengarry Glen Ross* (for which he won the Pulitzer Prize), and *Oleanna*. He has written four collections of essays, *Writing in Restaurants, Some Freaks, On Directing Film,* and *The Cabin* and his first novel *The Village* (Little, Brown) was published in 1994. He lives in Vermont and Massachusetts.

Friederike Mayröcker was born in 1924 in Vienna, where she still lives. In the 1960s, she was associated with the experimental Vienna Group, and she often collaborates with Ernst Jandl. She has received many literary prizes in both Austria and Germany, including the Theodor Körner Prize, the George Trakl Prize, and the Grosse Osterreichische Staatspreis. Other texts in translation can be found in *The Vienna Group: 6 Major Austrian Poets* (Station Hill) and *Heiligenanstalt* (No. 1 of *Dichten* =) (Burning Deck).

Jackie McAllister was born in Dundee, Scotland. Recent exhibitions of his work include those at the Thomas Nordanstad Gallery, New York (which represents him), and Galleri Tre, Stockholm, as well as a collaborative exhibition with Ross Knight, *Imi Knoebel or Evel Knievel?*, at American Fine Art Co., New York. He co-curated the Whitney Museum of American Art Co., 1988 exhibition *The Desire of the Museum* and curated *Travelogue-Reisetagebuch* (1993) in Vienna.

Carlo McCormick is the senior editor of *Paper* magazine. His book on multiple-personality disorder, *The Strange Case of T.L.*, will be published in April 1995 by Artspace.

Matt Mullican was born in Santa Monica, California in 1951. Recent one-person exhibitions include those at the Museum of Modern Art, New York, the La Jolla Museum, San Diego, the Rijksmuseum Kröller-Müller, The Netherlands, the M.I.T. List Center for the Visual Arts, Cambridge, Massachusetts, and Portikus, Frankfurt. His contributions to this issue are taken from a "virtual" city created in cooperation with Digital Editions in Hollywood. Mullican lives and works in New York, where he is represented by the Barbara Gladstone Gallery.

Joachim Neugroschel, who has won three PEN Translation Prizes and the translation prize of the French-American Foundation, has translated more than 140 books, including works by Paul Celan, Georges Bataille, and Elias Canetti.

Tony Oursler was born in New York in 1957. His recent solo exhibitions include those at Metro Pictures Gallery, New York, Portikus, Frankfurt, the Centre d'Art Contemporain, Geneva, and the Lisson Gallery, London. He has participated in group exhibitions at the Stedjelijk Museum,

Amsterdam, the 1989 Whitney Biennial, and Documenta 8, Kassel, Germany, among others. He lives and works in New York where he is represented by Metro Pictures Gallery.

Giuseppe Pontiggia was born in Como, Italy in 1934. He has published six works of fiction, including *La Morte in Banca* (1959) and *Vite di Uomini Non Illustri* (1993). As a critic, he has contributed to the *Corriere della Sera* and other periodicals, and has published two collections of essays. He lives in Milan.

Luis J. Rodriguez is director and founder of the Chicago-based Tia Chucha Press, a cross-cultural, socially engaged poetry publishing house. He is also an award-winning poet, critic, and journalist. His most recent book, *Always Running: La Vida Loca, Gang Days in L.A.* (Simon & Schuster/Touchstone) is a memoir of his life as a gang member from 1965–1973.

Aura Rosenberg has exhibited her photographs and sculpture throughout the United States and Europe. Recent exhibitions include those at the Neue Galerie in Graz, Austria, the Kunstlerhaus Bethanien, Berlin, the Centre Georges Pompidou, Paris, Terrain Gallery, San Francisco, and White Columns, New York. She lives and works in New York.

Jérôme Sans is an art critic and independent curator who has written extensively for contemporary art journals in Europe and the United States.

Peter Santino was born in 1948 in Kansas. He currently lives and works in Eureka, California. His work is represented by American Fine Art Co., New York.

Christian Schumann was born in Rhode Island in 1970. He received a B.F.A. from the San Francisco Art Institute in 1992 and he is represented in New York by Postmasters Gallery. His work will appear in the 1995 Whitney Biennial.

Birger Sellin was born in 1973. He currently lives with his family in Berlin, Germany.

Reginald Shepherd's book *Some Are Drowning* was recently published by the University of Pittsburgh Press. He is the 1994–95 Amy Lowell Traveling Scholar and a 1995 NEA Creative Writing Fellow.

Saul Steinberg lives in Manhattan and in Amagansett, Long Island. He is represented by the Pace Gallery, New York.

Paul Virilio is the director of the Ecole Spéciale d'Architecture in Paris. His books *The Aesthetics of Disappearance* (Autonomedia), *Lost Dimension* (Autonomedia), and *War and Cinema: The Logics of Perception* (Routledge), have been published in English.

Carol Volk's translation of *The New Ecological Order* by philosopher Luc Ferry will be published this spring by the University of Chicago Press. Also forthcoming are translations of a novel by Tahar Ben Jelloun called *The Broken Man* (The New Press) and two novels by Emmanuel Bove, *Night Departure* and *No Place* (Four Walls Eight Windows). She lives in New York.

Rosmarie Waldrop's most recent books of poems are *A Key Into the Language of America* (New Directions) and *Lawn of Excluded Middle* (Tender Buttons Press). Station Hill has published her novels *The Hanky of Pippin's Daughter* and *A Form/ of Taking/ It All*.

Robert Williams was born in Albuquerque, New Mexico in 1943. Along with Von Dutch Holland and Ed "Big Daddy" Roth, Williams was a pioneer of Southern California's "custom" car culture in the 1960s and an original contributor to *Zap Comix*. He is the founder and majority shareholder of *Juxtapoz* magazine. He has exhibited his work at the Museum of Contemporary Art, Los Angeles, the Laguna Art Museum, and Tony Shafrazi Gallery, New York. This year an exhibition of his prints will be traveling to Sydney and Tokyo and another exhibition will be held at Tamara Bane Gallery, Los Angeles, which represents his work. He is also represented by Bess Cutler Gallery, New York. He lives and works in North Hollywood, California.

David Young edits *FIELD*, a semiannual journal of poetry and poetics, and translates widely. His most recent book of poems is *Night Thoughts and Henry Vaughan*.

ILLUSTRATIONS

front cover Robert Williams, *Lord Solver Of Puzzledom*; Scholastic Designation: *They Brought Unto The Sage A Fraudulent Puzzle Calculated To Be Unsolvable And So After Contemplating For Three Days And Nights This Bogus Riddle, The Wise Man Pronounced The Jigsaw Game Not To Be The Mystery But Instead The Fools That Brought It*; Remedial Title: *An Idle Mind Will Find A Mystery In A Colostomy Bag*, detail, 1990. Oil on canvas, 30 x 36 in. Courtesy of the artist, Tamara Bane Gallery, Los Angeles, and Bess Cutler Gallery, New York.

back cover Jay DeFeo, *Untitled (Egyptian Collage)*, c. 1956. Photograph and game-board collage, $10^3/4$ x $12^1/4$ in. Courtesy of the Estate of Jay DeFeo.

title page Peter Santino, *762 Failures (Failure of Communication)*, detail, 1993. Courtesy of the artist and American Fine Art Co., New York.

pp. 13–16 Matt Mullican. Titles, dates, media, and dimensions listed below. Courtesy of the artist and the Barbara Gladstone Gallery, New York. **p. 13** *Untitled*, 1989. Ink jet printing on paper, 66 x 180 in. **pp. 14–15 (background)** *Untitled (Field Of Cities)*, 1990; **p. 15 (top)** *Untitled (Wall of History)*; and **p. 16** *Untitled (World Unframed Monument)*, 1989. Color dura-trans photographs and light box, ed. 5, all 36 x 48 in.

pp. 25–31 Peter Santino, *The Pleasure Of Failure*. Seven mixed media installations (titles and dates appear with illustrations, media and dimensions listed below). Courtesy of the artist and American Fine Art Co., New York.

pp. 25 and 26 (top and bottom) Tinted sand, dimensions variable.

p. 27 (top and bottom) Sand, dimensions variable.

p. 28 and 29 (top) Tinted sand, 10 ft. diameter.

p. 29 (bottom, left and right) Encaustic on wood, both $2^1/4$ in. diameter.

p. 30 Terra-cotta tile and cement, total dimensions variable.

p. 31 Terra-cotta tile, cement, and turf, dimensions variable.

p. 32 Georganne Deen, *Matchbook*, 1995. Gouache on matchbook, 2 x 2 x $3/8$ in. Courtesy of the artist. Photograph by Peter Berson.

pp. 35, 39, and 40 Dennis Hopper. Photographs by Annie Leibovitz.

pp. 36–37 Georganne Deen, *Map*, 1995. Ink and gouache on paper, 9 x 14 in. Courtesy of the artist.

pp. 42 and 44 Black-and-white photographs courtesy of Olie Anderson.

pp. 49–56 Robert Williams, *Cartoon Surrealism*. Eight oil on canvas paintings. Titles and dates appear with illustrations. Courtesy of the artist, Tamara Bane Gallery, Los Angeles, and Bess Cutler Gallery, New York. **pp. 49, 50, 54 (top and bottom), 55, 56** 30 x 36 in. **pp. 51 and 52–53** 20 x 24 in.

pp. 64–65, 68, 69, 72, 73, 76 (top and bottom) Photographs by Donna De Cesare. Titles and dates appear with illustrations. Black-and-white prints, 8 x 10 in. each. Courtesy of the artist.

p. 82 Christian Schumann, *For the Chess Garden*, 1995. Pencil on paper, $8^1/2$ x 11 in. Courtesy of the artist and Postmasters Gallery, New York.

pp. 96, 98 (bottom), 100 (bottom, left and right), 102 (bottom left) Courtesy of Photofest.

pp. 97, 102 (top), 104 (top), 105 (top and bottom), 106 (top and bottom), 108 (top), 108–109 Courtesy of The Bettmann Archive.

pp. 99 (top), 101, 108 (bottom) Courtesy of the Philadelphia Museum of Art.

pp. 98 (top), 99 (bottom), 102–103, 107 (top and bottom) Courtesy of AP/Worldwide Photos.

p. 100 (top) Photograph by Shigeko Kubota.

p. 104 (bottom) Photograph courtesy of the Metropolitan Museum of Art.

pp. 112–116 Aura Rosenberg, from the *Berliner Kindheit* series, 1995. Titles and dimensions below. Silver gelatin prints. Courtesy of the artist. **p. 112** *Carousel*, 10 x 8 in. **p. 114** *Butterfly Hunting*, 8 x 10 in. **p. 116** *Hide and Seek*, 10 x 8 in.

pp. 122–127 Chris Burden, *America's Darker Moments*. Titles, dates, and media appear with illustrations. Courtesy of the artist and the Gagosian Gallery, New York.

pp. 136–137 Saul Steinberg, *Las Vegas*, 1984. 11 x 14 in. each. Courtesy of the artist and the Pace Gallery, New York. **p. 136** *Poker Game*, colored pencil and pencil on paper. **p. 137** *Slot Machine*, pencil on paper.

pp. 138, 145, 152, 158 Photographs by Sibylle Bergemann. Courtesy of Ostkreuz, Berlin.

pp. 169–176 Tony Oursler, *Dummies, Flowers, and Alters*. Eight mixed media installations. Titles and dates appear with illustrations, media and dimensions listed below. Courtesy of the artist and Metro Pictures, New York.

p. 169 Cloth, green lamp, and video projection, 99 $1/2$ x 17 x 13 $1/2$ in. Photograph by John Riddy.

p. 170 Video projection, tripod, cloth, and light stand, dimensions variable. Performance by Tracy Leipold.

p. 171 Video projection, cloth, and mattress, dimensions variable. Performance by Tracy Leipold.

pp. 172–73 Video projection and cloth, 74 x 19 $1/2$ x 11 $3/4$ in. each. *Phobic* performance by Mike Kelley.

p. 174 (top) Video projection and cloth, dimensions variable. **(bottom)** Ink on paper, 8 $1/2$ x 11 in.

p. 175 Video projection and wood, 15 x 11 $1/2$ x 12 in.

p. 176 Video projection, silk flowers, tripod, and light stand, dimensions variable. Performance by Tracy Leipold.

pp. 225–232 Jay DeFeo, *A Conversation*. Eight works on paper. Titles, dates, media, and dimensions appear on **p. 224**. Courtesy of the Estate of Jay DeFeo, Kohn Turner Gallery, Los Angeles, and Nicole Klagsbrun, New York.

p. 246 Anonymous misinformation posted in lower Manhattan, February 1995. Ink on cardboard, 18 x 12 in.

"If magazines still exist 20 years from now,
you can bet a lot more of them will be international.
And the literary ones are likely to resemble
an attractive new quarterly from Prague
called *Trafika*." —*The Washington Post*

Trafika

19 years ahead of its time.

Subscription of four issues annually, $35

A v a i l a b l e   n o w   a t   o v e r   6 1 9   b o o k s t o r e s   w o r l d w i d e

Further information in the US:
TRAFIKA
Post Office Box 250413, Columbia Station, New York, NY 10025-1536

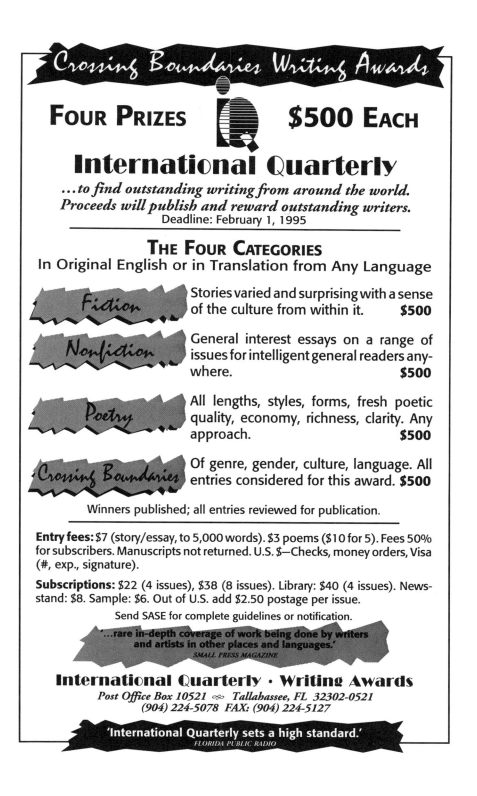

Grand Street would like to thank
the following for their generous support:

Cathy and Stephen Graham
Barbara Howard
The National Endowment for the Arts
Suzanne and Sanford J. Schlesinger
Betty and Stanley K. Sheinbaum

Back Issues of Grand Street

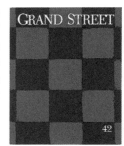

An Indispensable Collection

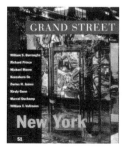
Now Available–Order While They Last

CALL 1-800-807-6548 or send name, address, issue number(s), and quantity.
American Express, Mastercard, and Visa accepted; please send credit card number and
expiration date. Back issues are $15.00 each ($18.00 overseas and Canada),
including postage and handling, payable in U.S. dollars.
Address orders to *Grand Street* Back Issues, 131 Varick Street, Suite 906, New York, N.Y. 10013.

The bookstores where

GRAND STREET

can be found include:

GRAND STREET

David Mamet
Robert Williams
Dennis Hopper
Saul Steinberg
Paul Virilio
Chris Burden
Walter Benjamin

Games

52

Black Oak Books, Berkeley, CA
Bookstore Fiona, Carson, CA
University of California Books, Irvine, CA
Museum of Contemporary Art,
    Los Angeles, CA
Diesel Books, Oakland, CA
Logos, Santa Cruz, CA
Arcana, Santa Monica, CA
Small World Books, Venice, CA
Stone Lion Books, Fort Collins, CO
Yale Co-op, New Haven, CT
University of Connecticut Bookstore,
    Storrs, CT
Bookworks, Washington, DC
Oxford Bookstore, Atlanta, GA
Iowa Book & Supply, Iowa City, IA
Prairie Lights, Iowa City, IA
University Books, Iowa City, IA
Seminary Co-op, Chicago, IL
Von's Book Shop, West Lafayette, IN
Carmichael's, Louisville, KY
Waterstone's Books, Boston, MA
M.I.T. Press Bookstore, Cambridge, MA
Nantucket Books, Nantucket, MA
Broadside Books, Northampton, MA
Provincetown Books, Provincetown, MA
Books Etc., Portland, ME
Book Beat, Oak Park, MI
Baxter's Books, Minneapolis, MN

Walker Art Center Books, Minneapolis, MN
Hungry Mind Bookstore, St. Paul, MN
Whistler's, Kansas City, MO
Left Bank Books, St. Louis, MO
Nebraska Bookstore, Lincoln, NE
Dartmouth Books, Hanover, NH
Micawber Books, Princeton, NJ
Salt of the Earth, Albuquerque, NM
Collected Works, Santa Fe, NM
Community Books, Brooklyn, NY
Talking Leaves, Buffalo, NY
Book Revue, Huntington, NY
The Bookery, Ithaca, NY
Doubleday Books, New York, NY
Gotham Book Mart, New York, NY
St. Mark's Bookstore, New York, NY
Wendell's Books, New York, NY
UC Bookstore, Cincinnati, OH
Books & Co., Dayton, OH
Looking Glass Books, Portland, OR
Farley's Bookshop, New Hope, PA
Bradd Alan Books, Philadelphia, PA
Joseph Fox Books, Philadelphia, PA
College Hill, Providence, RI
Chapter Two Books, Charleston, SC
Open Book, Greenville, SC
Xanadu Bookstore, Memphis, TN
DiverseBooks, Houston, TX
Sam Weller's, Salt Lake City, UT
Williams Corner, Charlottesville, VA
Studio Art Shop, Charlottesville, VA
Northshire Books, Manchester, VT
Woodland Patter, Milwaukee, WI